D1607145

Contents

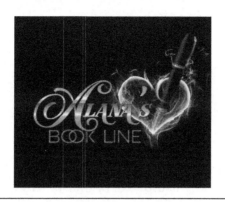

DYCE
An Urban Romance
By
A.Lana

Female Cover Model: IG _itsladyyy

Lady is a female rapper from Bompton Ca. Her debut For Me "Sandman" which climbed the charts within weeks. Check her out on all platforms.

DYCE

Dyce

A. Lana

Introduction

Stormy had made a promise to her mother that she'd walk away from a Hood Love. A love that could be dangerous not only for her but those she most cares about. The heart wants what it wants, and although she made the promise to leave his type alone, she needed Deon's love like she needed air in her lungs.

In one night, Stormy's whole world came crashing down; resentment settled in and from that day forward, she despised her father and every man like him.

She left the hood at the first chance she got to find the life her mother believed she deserved. Although they were from two different walks of life, Stormy knew at first sight that Blake Whitman was the one. The way he loved on his black queen was the confirmation she needed— hood love is not it!!

What happens when she runs into the rich, cocky, and handsome Lloyd Dyce? Stormy knows he's connected to the same lifestyle that left her bitter and broken, plus she has a good man now, so she wants no parts.

Lloyd disregards Stormy's disinterest in him along with her relationship with the white boy. He's determined to snatch her into his web. He would decide what will happen between the two of them when the time comes.

Julius is living two different lives. When in Cali, he's a dangerous hood icon with a surfer swag. But when in Florida attending school, he's a nerdy white boy. Staying focused on his studies keeps him grounded. Being a part of his parents' empire is a must; he was born into it. Once he obtains his degree though, he plans to walk away and settle down with a good girl. However, he slips up and falls for the opposite. The only problem is this chick isn't interested in a nerd. She loves dudes with money and expensive cars. His gut is telling him to stay away from the potential headache, but his heart wants her by any means necessary. Will he have to reveal J-White to her in hopes of winning her heart? Or will he ignore his desire to be with her and continue being Julius?

Supported by an intriguing set of characters, Dyce will make you cross your fingers praying your favorite character HIT DICE!

Prologue

"The best revenge is not to fuck with him. And show his ass you ain't pressed."

"What's up, Stormy?" Deon's handsome ass spoke as he walked up to me. Candy and I were sitting at the picnic table talking about how we didn't want to go to school the next day.

"Huh, oh, hey," I spoke shyly, fumbling around with my hands.

"Can I talk to you for a minute?" He asked, gesturing with his head while looking at Candy like he wanted her to step off. She didn't catch the hint. She was just as surprised as I was. Deon nor his friends talked to us; they hung out with girls their age. "Let's talk over here," Deon ushered, grabbing me by the hand, and we began to walk off.

I could've died. The cutest boy in the neighborhood was holding my hand. Now, don't get me wrong, I was cute but only eleven years old; too young for a fourteen-year-old. OG Goat aka my dad, popped in my head. Nervously, I scanned the park for daddy. His car was gone, and momma was standing next to her red drop-top Mustang talking with her friends.

"One day, you are going to be my girl. You too young now." Deon advised, causing my head to snap back toward him so quick I heard my neck crack. "You hear me?"

I was blown over him, saying I would be his girl; I was looking everywhere but at him.

"Look at me. What I'm about to tell you is important."

I glared into his eyes, giving him my full attention.

"Your daddy is big in the dope game. My mom's push weight too." He lingered.

Of course, I knew what my dad did. No one flat out told me, it was something that I learned over the years of being around him and listening to people talk.

He continued, "You fly, and I'm fly." He glanced down at his J's and then at the Rolex chain on my neck. "Your dad got more money than my mom, but my mom grinds hard, so she is going to come up too. Then, after her, it'll be me." His confidence reminded me of my dad's. Or was it cockiness? My mom referred to dad as both often.

I batted my long lashes, unsure of what I was to say, if anything.

"One day, I am going to be big in the game like your pops. I'll probably take over his spot. When I do, I need you on my side. You already know what it's like to have money, so I ain't got to worry about you just being with me for clout. We are getting married. We are going to be the most fly couple out here. What do you think?"

Where I come from, it was typical for the kids to wanna gain wealth by being a dope dealer. So, I didn't think anything bad about it; I was ecstatic to be his girl.

"K." I answered.

"When you turn fifteen, I'm going to make it official. But right now, you are still my girl. You can't talk to nobody, you hear me?"

I nodded my head yes.

"Nah, I need to hear it."

"Yes," I said.

"Good girl," he kissed me on the forehead and strolled off but quickly doubled back.

"Oh, and this is between us. This is a test to see if I can trust you."

"Ok." I blushed.

I wasn't about to break my man's trust. When Candy asked what we talked about, I told her that he wanted to date me but found out I was too young.

"I'm old enough." She replied. And I cut my eyes at her.

She didn't seem like she cared. She changed the subject. I wasn't listening to anything she talked about; I was still trying to digest Deon and I's future.

For four years I had to pretend like the love of my life wasn't my future husband. I had to watch him date other girls. I cried for two days when I heard about him going to the prom with the neighborhood hoe. When he would catch me alone, he'd hug me so tight and tell me how he couldn't wait for us to be together. And that he could get in trouble with the police or have worse consequences if my dad found out about us. His kisses on my forehead and our late-night talks on the phone, I would look forward to.

We've only been official for a year, and now all of a sudden, it's over? Deon dumped me like I never meant anything to him. What happened to the promises he made me?

This heartbreak I wouldn't wish on my worst enemy. I wanted to scream, cry, kick, and pull my braids from my scalp one minute. The next, I felt like dropping to the floor on my knees and begging God to change his mind. Make him admit that breaking up with me was a big mistake and that he didn't want to do it in the first place. He didn't even have to tell me he was sorry, I just wanted him to come back to me.

"I cannot believe I am going through this," I cried as I paced back and forth in my bedroom. "Like, dude, I am only sixteen years old. I should not be going through this." Wiping the tears from my eyes, I marched over to the windowpane and gazed into the backyard. My sad orbs rested on the swimming pool. The light inside the pool reflected on the 3ft mark. It was there, standing in 3ft where Deon and I shared our first real kiss. I pouted, turning around staring at the purple comforter on my queen size bed. The same bed not even a month ago, where I gave him my virginity. That visual once gave me butterflies. Now, all I wanted to do was cry when I reflected on that moment.

"It's your fault you are going through this. You have no reason to. There are too many niggas out here that want you." Candy's harsh statement pulled me from my thoughts.

"Really?" I turned around and looked at my play cousin. Candy was sitting at my computer desk, rocking back and forth in the chair. Light, bright girl with a head full of sandy brown hair that she wore in two thick braids going to the back. Her nose was sprinkled with freckles. Candy was cute but her attitude could be disgusting sometimes.

"Yes, Stormy. If the boy said he doesn't want to be with you, he doesn't want to be with you. Fuck him. You act like you are one of these ugly, dusty-ass girls out here. You are not desperate. Stop acting like it." She shook her head. "I know you love him, but if he said he doesn't want to be with you, then let it be. The best revenge is not to fuck with him. And show his ass you ain't pressed." She stated matter of factly, rolling her eyes and pursing her lips.

"Deon loves me. I know he does." I spoke with certainty, and I wasn't just saying that either. He loved the fuck out of me. He's told me plenty of times. We loved each other. I was his future. I have been for years. "It's my daddy's fault. That's the problem." My voice cracked. I couldn't bear to think about not being with Deon.

"Look, cousin, if he gave a fuck about you, then he wouldn't have chosen money over you. A person who loves you wouldn't put anything above you. Uncle Moe taught me that. And that's why I ain't trying to go there with no man. Love is a game to them. I will

12

never let a nigga play me. After watching y'all depressed when you get dumped I know for a fact that's not how I wanna be. I'm good on love." She declared, folding her arms across her chest.

"Wow!" I replied, fluttering my eyes. Candy was so cold.

"Ain't no wow, you control your emotions. You don't have to feel like you are feeling. It's a choice."

Waving my hand at her negative energy, I flopped down on the bed, aggressively wiping more tears from my eyes. I refused to go back and forth with a person who had never been in love. Candy didn't know what the hell she was talking about.

"Knock...Knock....,"

my mother's sweet voice announced from behind the door; she peeped her head in before fully entering the room. She was still dressed in pink nursing scrubs. No matter how tired she was before she retired for the night, she came into my room to check on me. We would talk about my day, I would ask about hers. Then, before she departed, she would tuck me in and leave me with a kiss on the lips. You would hardly ever see her not smiling. People say she had a warm, loving spirit. She's beautiful too. We shared the same toffee skin tone, tight eyes, and high cheekbones. Ma had that good hair. She could wet it and go on about her business. My mane was soft and long.

"Hey, Candy." Mom greeted, looking at her.

"Hi, auntie." Candy replied with a smile and a wave. Like she just wasn't giving her daughter a hard time about being in love. Momma made her way over to where I was and stood in front of me.

"What's wrong, Stormy?" she asked, her hand caressing my cheek.

"Mommy, I'm heartbroken." My voice cracked, and another flood of tears trickled down my cheeks.

She got down on her knees and pulled me into her arms, wrapping them around me tight. I broke down in her bosom. It hurt so bad. It felt like my heart had been ripped from my chest and stomped on with Timberland boots. At times I barely could breathe. I was drowning in pain praying that Deon would rescue me soon. If I knew heartbreak felt like this, I don't think I would have ever submitted to love .

"It hurts. I know it does. I can't say I know what you are going through, but I know when you care deeply about a person, it hurts to let go."

"What do I do?" I asked hopelessly, looking up at her. I could feel a panic attack coming.

"Stormy, I think you should look at Deon breaking things off as a blessing." She advised with a warm smile.

I searched her eyes not sure if she was serious or not. This was the first time I heard her say such a thing. I wasn't sure why she was saying it now. I didn't want to hear that. I looked away, my eyes landed on my bookshelf.

"Look at me," she insisted, turning my head back toward her.

"Deon is living a life I don't want you involved in. I'm a wife of a hustler, and that shit is hell. You are constantly worried about their well-being. If they are in jail or, worse , dead. They will promise you that they will never let anything happen to you, and you want to believe that. However, thoughts of home invasions, someone coming after you or your child will keep you up at night." She confessed. "I don't know his reason for breaking up with you, but I respect it. You can do better and a hustler, ain't it. Everyone has this perfect illusion of what a hood love is." She stood up, shaking her head. "Trust me; it's not it. "

I loved my mom with all my heart. I loved our talks and coming to her about anything, but I wasn't feeling what she was saying. My eyes darted toward Candy, who was nodding her head, agreeing with my mom.

"Let it go now. If he's killed or goes to prison the pain will be much worse . The longer you stay the harder it'll be if this lifestyle takes him away from you."

"But mom."

"I know."

My mother asked for a hug and told me to get myself together. She bid Candy and me goodnight before she left out the room. I avoided looking at Candy, who I could feel staring at me.

"We going to the party or not?" Candy asked, breaking the awkward silence .

Parties have never been my thing, but I knew Deon would be there, and since he wasn't answering my calls, I had to address him there.

"Yeah, we going," I answered, with my lips pursed, making my way to my closet to find something to shit on him in.

" I'll be back to get you in a few. Be ready." Candy grabbed her things and left.

"I sure will."

Deon

Bitch, I don't want you. What the fuck part of that you don't understand?

"Nigga we did that shit. On god, we about to take over this shit. Get these old heads up out of here." My boy Naz said, all hype and shit. The nigga couldn't even sit down, been pacing back and forth for the last ten minutes.

"You already know. As long as we stick to the plan, nobody will ever suspect us. Next summer, we announce our take over." I explained, standing up from the kitchen table headed toward the living room. Naz trailed behind.

"OH, I'm listening. Nigga, you have taught me patience is a mutha fucking virtue. Damn." He shook his head. Naz couldn't believe how I made it easy to rob my boss. The Kilos we took was just what we needed to take over the streets.

He was right, patience was a virtue. It was hard to look into that nigga Goat's face while he tried to school me on how to become a hustler knowing I didn't have respect for him. My momma had taught me the game since I was a little nigga in grade school. She knew she would have to leave one day; it comes with the hustle. When the day came, she wanted to make sure I was equipped with the right tools to continue her legacy. I wasn't about to let her down either.

"Go to the pad and get dressed," I suggested, looking at Naz. There was a party in the hood, and we were there.

"Bet." He retorted trekking to the front door. I chuckled, we been boys since grade school, and I still got a kick out of how bowleg he was. The bitches loved that shit.

We agreed to meet at Burger Palace so our crew could caravan.

As I headed to my bedroom, I glimpsed at my mother's picture on the wall and smiled. Queeny will always be my hero. My momma was that bitch and while she was away, I would continue to make her that bitch.

The vibration in my jeans caused me to retrieve my cellphone from my front pocket. I grimaced when I saw Stormy's name. She called and texted so much I decided I was going to get a new cellphone. Our breakup wasn't supposed to be this soon but now that I made my move on her pops, I didn't need her anymore. I can't say I didn't have feelings for Stormy because I did. However, I didn't let them get as deep as she believed they were. As a young nigga I was trained to use Stormy to get close to her pops. I found my own way, so I didn't need her anymore. I hit decline on her call and turned my phone off. She was fucking annoying. Bitch, I don't want you. What the fuck part of that you don't understand?

All I do is WIN, win, win, no matter what

Got money on my mind I can never get enough And every time I step in the building Everybody hands go up And they stay there And they say -yeah And they stay there

All I do is WIN blared from the speakers of my grey Impala SS, we filed out of our whips three cars deep. It was six of us-all niggas. We all circled my car singing my hood anthem. Blunts were in the air, blue cups filled with Grey goose in our hands, and all eyes were on us. If they thought we were stunting now, wait until next summer when we introduce MY crew to the streets.

"Nigga, I can get used to this." Naz said, laughing.

"You may as well, 'cause we ain't going nowhere no time soon. Bet that." I assured him, taking a gulp from my cup. My eyes landed on the four other niggas that was in our crew. They worked for Goat too, but soon would be on my payroll. Like, a father , I watched everyone in action tonight. I would be studying their moves over the months to come.

"I got a feeling that nigga is going to be a problem," Naz said, looking toward this nigga Bishop. I wasn't worried about his fat ass.

"All problems get eliminated. The way we are about to take over even our haters are gonna wanna be on our team." I boasted.

"And take over is what we about to do." Naz cosigned.

Naz and I slapped hands.

We chilled a little longer outside of the party before we mobbed inside the yard. I caught a glimpse of two white girls pulling up in a drop-top Mercedes. They damn sure wasn't from our block. I made a mental note to stay far away from the hoes. They'll never put a case on me.

Stormy

Forever and always.

"You look cute little girl," my mom admired. I had just walked down the stairs and into the living room. Mom was coming out of the kitchen dressed in a housecoat and slippers with a bowl of crunch berries in her hand.

"Thank you," I blushed, turning around to model.

We both giggled.

"You are so silly, little girl. You wearing those jeans with your cute self."

"I get it from my momma." I teased.

"That you did," she snorted, taking a spoon of cereal into her mouth.

I did get my looks from my mother. Pretty in the face and body that I was forever getting compliments on. Average size breasts, flat stomach, wide hips, and juicy thighs. I looked good in everything, but these jeans had my plump bottom sitting up and sticking out extra like my momma's. I was feeling myself while rocking a pair of denim ripped blue jeans, a white crop top, and black heels to match my black rhinestone belt. Sunday night, my mother touched up the gold highlights in my hair and flat ironed it. My red acrylic nails matched my red matt lipstick. I was super cute.

"So, you decided to go to the party?" she questioned, already knowing the answer.

THE FRONT DOOR OPENED before I could answer her, our eyes fell on my father. We watched as he stormed into the house. He didn't even look at us. Any other time I would be happy to see his handsome face, but I was upset with him. I blamed him for the way Deon was treating me. Daddy had recently welcomed Deon to his crew. He was officially a hustler, running with the big boys. I know for a fact my dad told him he had to stay away from me. He was overprotective that way. Plus, he would always say none of the dudes in the hood were good enough for me. That is the only thing that makes sense.

"Well, hello, husband." My mother spoke.

"What's up?" Daddy retorted, making his way to the bar. We watched as he poured a glass of Hennessy, taking it back and putting the glass back down, making a clinking sound. My mother looked at me with a warm smile. I could see the concern on her face.

"Well, you have fun. I mean it. Enjoy yourself. Nothing else matters."

"Where are you going?" Dad asked, heading for the stairs.

"To a party with Candy," I muttered.

"I don't like that red lipstick." He barked.

"I do," I replied, kissing my teeth.

"And I like it too," my mom cut in , coming to my defense.

He shook his head and headed up the stairs. Something was definitely wrong, but it wasn't my business. All I cared about was getting to this party and checking Deon's ass.

"Have fun and be safe." He yelled from up the stairs.

Bonnnkkkkk…

"That's Candy," I announced at the sound of her horn. I kissed my mom on the cheek and turned to leave.

She lightly grabbed my hand, causing me to look at her.

"Do not force yourself on anyone. Have fun, Stormy. Trust me when I say you do not want to be connected to a man like Deon." She looked up the stairs and then back at me, whispering, "I love my husband, but If I had to do it all over again, I would find myself a nice corporate man. I would have listened to my mom." She smiled, but I could see the hurt in her eyes. My grandmother whom I never met when brought up made my mother sad. For the first time, I felt my mother was unhappy. It made me sad. I always thought she and my father were the perfect couple. Tonight, I feel different. She sat her bowl on the coffee table, pulled me into a bear hug and squeezed me tight, rocking me from side to side. In her arms, I felt safe, like everything would be alright as long as I had her. I could've stayed in her arms all night. I may not have liked the realness of her words, but I knew they were coming from a place of love. She didn't want to see me disappointed like her. She wanted her daughter happy.

"I promise I will have fun. I will not worry about someone who isn't worrying about me." I proclaimed , pulling away. Candy had honked again.

"Good." She kissed me on my forehead. We said our I love yous. As I walked out the door, an eerie feeling came over me. Suddenly, I felt down. My heart was heavy. My mother's revelation darkened my spirit. Stepping onto the porch, the warm breeze embraced me. I turned around and looked at my mother one last time.

"I love you."

"I love you too, sweetheart. Forever and always."

He got me Fuck'd Up.

I know I promised my mother that I would have fun and not worry about a person who wasn't worried about me, but hell no; Deon had me all the way messed up. How was he just going to be in the same vicinity as me and ignore me? I was determined to have an enjoyable time, and it was working at first. When Deon and his crew walked in, everything changed. All the emotions and feelings I tried to suppress came rushing back. I wanted my man back. How could I allow Mr. Right to leave me?

Deon was donned in a black jean outfit and white Air Force ones. He got a fresh hair cut---waves sick. I even noticed a new chain around his neck. I couldn't take my eyes off him. When the crew stepped in, they stole the attention of everybody that was at the party. Deon was already popular in the hood due to his good looks and the way he dressed. His mother was a hustler but has been locked up for a couple of years now. Deon followed in her footsteps and took on life as a hustler. And within a few months, he was like a hood celebrity to our generation.

"I need another shot," I said to Candy, who was looking at pictures some guy was showing her on his phone.

"Deon here now you want to get drunk?" She tossed, without looking my way.

I rolled my eyes and stormed off back into the house. I didn't appreciate how she was being so judgmental, and I had planned to tell her about that shit too.

I made it into the kitchen, glad no one was near the spiked punch because I didn't feel like talking. I grabbed a red plastic cup and the scooping spoon and

25

made myself a full glass. I counted to three in my head before I gulped it down, damn near finishing it.

"Slow down," a deep voice said from behind.

"Mind your business," I replied angrily, kissing my teeth at Joe, our school's star football player.

"Girl, you going to get drunk. And besides, ladies sip."

"Well, sip your shit," I replied heatedly and stormed off. I was drunk already; I could feel it.

When I made it back outside I noticed Deon standing near a dice game, more than likely ready to join. I stomped over to where he was.

"I need to talk to you," I spat, one hand on my hip.

He gave me the once over before looking back at the game. The way he was handling me hurt my feelings. He was tripping.

"So, you going to stand there and ignore me, Deon?" I yelled, voice cracking. I felt the stares, and I didn't care. Deon has always been low-key real laid back, so I'm sure he wasn't feeling the attention. "Deon. You hear me?"

He snatched me by the arm and practically yanked me across the yard and out of the gate to his car. Then, pushed me against the driver's door. His six-foot frame hovered over me.

"What you gotta say?" He spoke through tight teeth, eyes hard.

"Why are you doing me like this?" I sobbed.

"Man Stormy," he growled and turned to walk away. I pulled him back by his jacket.

"Stop walking away from me. You are acting like a coward." I screamed.

"Watch your mouth." He warned.

"It's the truth. I gave you my heart. I gave you a piece of me I'll never get back, and this how you do me? Fuck me? I don't mean shit to you. Huh?" I cried. I didn't care who saw me.

"What part don't you understand? I don't want to be with you." He bellowed.

As soon as the words left his mouth my hand went across his face. I am sure everyone at the party heard the sound it made.

"Stop lying. Stop lying, and you do. You're just saying that because of the deal you have with my father. You choose that life over me?"

I watched as he looked around with a scowl on his face. His chest rose up and down. He was pissed. So, was I.

"Get in the car Stormy." He demanded. "Now." He bellowed.

I stomped over to the passenger side of his vehicle and climbed inside. Deon was already in the driver's seat. He glared at me.

"When a mutha fucka tell you they don't want you accept that shit. That shit is weak. I am not the man for you, and I do not wanna be with you. Graduate, go off to college, go find a man that's on your level. This my last time telling you, I don't want you." He jumped out the car and slammed the door.

"But I'm... noooo. You said you loved me. It was us until the end. We belong together." I sobbed.

I sat in the car in my feelings crying hoping Deon would come back and say something to make me feel better. When the car door opened, I was hopeful, but it was nobody but Candy.

"Get the fuck up out this niggas whip. You are embarrassing us."

"Leave me alone." I pouted.

"Stormy, let's go; you are doing too much." Candy fussed, yanking me out of the car.

I didn't want to leave, I wanted to act a damn fool. If I didn't think Candy would call my momma and snitch on me, I would have done some shit to make Deon wanna leave too. I looked around; he went back into the party. He didn't care about me.

"Weak bitches," I heard a chick say. I looked to my left and two white girls dressed like sluts in their mini dresses were looking at me like I stank.

"What?" Candy and I said in unison.

"A blind person could see that he doesn't want you, why keep trying? Being desperate is not attractive." Red head spat bitterly.

I pulled my hand away from Candy's and stormed over to her. With a closed fist I punched that hoe dead in her mouth.

"Oh my god." Her friend screamed.

Cany yanked her, by the hair, she fell to the ground.

"Go the fuck back to white Ville." Candy yelled.

"Stupid bitch." I roared, kicking her in the ass.

"Let's go, they are known for calling the police." Candy pulled me by the arm.

I could hear laughter as the two of us made it to Candy's car. It took everything for me not to run back and take all my anger and frustration out on her. She better be glad I didn't want to go to jail.

The moment I flopped in the seat I cried again. I had a feeling the pain wouldn't leave anytime soon.

———

Everything was a blur. I didn't even know when we arrived at my house until Candy spoke.

"You need me to come in with you?" Candy inquired. We pulled into my driveway.

I shook my head no. Grabbing my purse from the backseat, I climbed out of the car. My vision was blurry from the tears. I was in a daze. Fumbling in my purse and retrieving my keys, I got ready to put them in the door when I noticed it was already open. I felt it was odd in the back of my mind, but I still entered the house, shutting and locking the door behind me. When I made it to the front of the stairs, I turned on the light switch nearest to the stairway then took the stairs slowly because I was still troubled about what went down between Deon and me. Once I made it to the top of our staircase, I heard my father sobbing. He was screaming and begging for help. My heart sank to the pit of my stomach. I suddenly couldn't breathe. Too afraid of what I would see, I stood frozen trying to steady my breathing. His cries pierced my soul. The more he yelled the harder it was for me to take a step. I knew it was something wrong with my mother, but I didn't know what. Suddenly something took over my body, and I darted toward the room. I wasn't fucking prepared. I just knew what I was seeing had to be a nightmare.

"What happened?" I cried as I stared on in disbelief. Blood dripped from my father's head while he cried over my mother.

"No, No. No. Please wake up, babe. Please don't leave us." He howled.

"What happened?" I cried again, standing behind him. I will never forget how he looked at me—with so much sorrow. There was no life in his eyes.

"They killed her. They killed her. My wife is gone."

10-years later

Lloyd

I was relaxed on a lawn chair in my back yard getting topped off. Between the beautiful sunny day and superb head, I felt great.

"Fuck, just like that," I instructed, my hands where tangled in her hair. My toes curled. The slurping sounds paired with the head of my dick touching her tonsils I was about to bust. The got damn phone vibrating back-to-back was pissing me the fuck off. I continued to fuck her in the mouth until I exploded. Fuuuccckkkk." I bellowed; Jamie drank all my seeds. I could feel the tension from my shoulders release. "Thanks bae." I told her, grabbing my phone. Seeing Bishop's number my heart sank. The last I knew my baby brother was out here with him. What the fuck was going on? I immediately called him back.

"Yo." I greeted, putting my dick back into my pants.

I listened to what Bishop had to say. The tension was back. Pissed was an understatement after hearing the news he delivered. I jumped up from the chair, ignoring Jamie and making my way into the house. My fucking brother was in trouble.

It was a gorgeous sunny day in Cali, but the news I received made it seem like a cold night. Instead of sitting back relaxing in my backyard while enjoying the weather, it felt like I was racing on a foggy night. I was like a volcano ready to erupt. This is the shit I was trying to avoid. I swear this little nigga is hardheaded as fuck. My brother and I warned this idiot about these grimy streets and young hoes.

Stopping abruptly in front of the commercial building, I killed the engine on my foreign. I didn't need the strap, but out of habit, I snatched it from the center console-anyway. Once my Gucci loafers hit the pavement, I secured my Glock. 9 on my waist.

I could feel my blood steaming, my mind hurtling.

I rushed toward the office entrance and in through the glass double doors. Lemon-scented Lysol in the air, a total of four chairs in the waiting area-two on each side--- all empty. Light Jazz is playing in the background. A security guard was posted on the side of the receptionist's desk next to an artificial palm tree fucking around on his phone. Sitting behind a white and gold desk was a fine-ass receptionist. Her brown tight eyes were on me. That was my first time seeing her. Her beauty was hypnotizing. I had to do a double-take—flawless creamy toffee skin. A pretty white smile paired with the perfect set of pink lips. Why in the fuck was I thinking about how I'd lick that mole sitting on her lower lip? It was shaped like a cloud. So. Cute. At the sound of her voice, my eyes darted back to hers, wondering if she found me attractive like most women.

I'm standing at 6'3, with an athletic build. Whisky colored complexion with eyes that change from a dark blue to dark grey. Today , they are grey. No ink on my body, I didn't do needles. Long dreads and a beard I kept nice and neat. The women consider me a god.

The plaque on her desk read Stormy.

"Welcome to Ross & Ross. Do you have an appointment?" She inquired, not a hint of lust in her eyes. I wasn't feeling that.

Peeling my eyes away, I grimaced as I mobbed on past both her and the sucka ass security.

"Excuse me, sir." She called out.

Two at a time, I took the stairs to the second floor.

"Excuse me, sir, I have to check you in." The soft voice called behind me.

Slowly turning around, my eyes scanned her curvy body from toe to head. She was dressed in black Tory Burch flats, a pinstriped skirt, and a white blouse with a diamond pendant on the right. Her hair was in one of them messy buns with two Chinese sticks at the top of her head.

"Yo, bro. You can't go up there." Security yelled, taking a step.

I chuckled, turned, and kept walking. In my opinion, he wasn't talking about shit. I already knew he wasn't stupid enough to try to stop me physically, but if by chance I'm wrong, that was his ass.

With no fucks given , I barged right into my lawyer's office. His fat ass was sitting behind the oak wood desk, rocking in his oversized brown leather chair—cellphone to his ear. You could almost see smoke coming from his ears at the sight of my no-manners having ass.

"Let me call you back," he said to whoever was on the phone and hung up. Face beet red. His glare isn't hard as mine tho.

"How can I help you?" he asked as calmly as he could.

"Why the fuck is my brother in jail with no bail? And why in the fuck haven't you called me to tell me he was in jail?" I bellowed, quickly sliding my hands into the pockets of my slacks. I stood there gawking. His reply would determine whether my hands stayed tucked. If it wasn't for the fuck nigga who was with him when he was arrested, I probably still wouldn't know what was up.

"I just got off the phone with a judge. As a favor owed to my family, she will handle everything. Your brother should have bail within a few hours." He explained.

"Why wasn't I called in the first place?" I snarled.

"You pay me to handle things. When he called me, I began to do my job. Was I to call you and say your brother was arrested for the rape of the chief of police's daughter?" He countered.

I grimaced. Hearing that shit made me sick to my stomach. I can't believe this kid got himself into this bullshit.

Gazing out of the picture window behind the desk, looking at the busy downtown traffic, I was in deep thought. Trying to figure out how this happened. Ross told me how he would handle everything and call when Julius was released.

"Lloyd." He yelled, pulling me from my stupor.

"Yeah. You do that. Call me as soon as you have him."

"Will do," he assured me, standing up from his chair. I watched as he walked around his desk and to the door, holding it open, glaring at me.

"Get the fuck out of my office. Don't ever barge into my got damn office again." Voice bouncing off the walls.

"My bad," I replied sarcastically.

"Yeah. You better be glad I'm in a good mood, or else your rude ass would be the reason I fire the two downstairs." He chuckled, "not like you care."

"Who's the chick?" I quipped.

"She's taken and get this." He looked out the door and back at me. "She doesn't date black men." He muttered with a wink.

I gave him a reverse nod before leaving his office. Taking the stairs to exit, I didn't even bother to look the receptionist's way on my way out. Women like her left a nasty ass taste in my mouth. I take it she doesn't think she's black either.

Later that evening

"Babe, why aren't you dressed?" Jamie, my fiancé, asked her hands on her nonexistent hips, head slightly tilted to the side, looking up at me with those tight eyes. Jamie was dressed in a black evening gown that complimented her vanilla skin tone. She wore her hair in one braid down the middle with gold beads on the sides. In her ears were the 3carat diamond studs I got her last year. Besides lip-gloss and long mink lashes, her face was bare. A beautiful woman she was.

"You look nice," I said. Grabbing an apple from the fruit dish, I continued out of the kitchen.

"I would like to return the compliment, but you aren't dressed." She retorted; I could feel her coming up behind me.

"I ain't going." I tossed over my shoulder, biting the apple.

"So, that's what we are doing now? Canceling plans with no explanation?" Stopping in my tracks just at the entrance of the kitchen, I took a deep breath and let it out. Usually, when I say something, it's final. No explanation is needed because I run shit. However, this is her aunt's birthday party. Though they were related through marriage and Michelle wasn't with her uncle any longer, they were extremely close. I admired that, and when Michelle wasn't getting on my nerves, I liked her too. However, I didn't mess with her folks like that and didn't feel like being bothered. Even if it was to satisfy my lady. I spun around.

"Jamie, I got a lot of shit going on right now. Tell Michelle I got the flu or something. Lie or not." I suggested with a shrug.

She tossed her hands in the air,

"I can't believe this. Why are you always doing this to me? I know you don't like them, but what about me, do you at least care about me?" she cried, dropping her hands to her sides, "you always talk about loyalty, and how you will always do-right by people that do right by you. Damn, after all this time, I get nothing. You don't care just a little bit?" Tears ran down her face as she stood waiting on an answer.

With one stride, I was up on her pulling her into my chest. The kiss I planted on her forehead only caused her to cry harder. The problem was I didn't care. I had love for my fiancé, but I wasn't in love, don't think I'll ever be.

"Have fun; tell Michelle I owe her one. Pick a spot, preferably an island. I'm there." I pulled away and headed out of the kitchen.

I know me not attending the party still had her in her feelings, and I didn't care. I suggested the getaway, not out of guilt but an obligation. Jamie is right; I do value loyalty. I am a man that believes in returning the same energy the next person gives. And most importantly, you never want to be despised by someone loyal to a fault.

For some odd reason, my thoughts drifted to Ross's receptionist. I wondered if she ever dated black men and if so, why did she stop. It had to be something deep-rooted. Why I gave a fuck, I didn't know.

Stormy

"Hello?" I answered annoyed as ever. This was like the fourth time today that I received a call from someone with the wrong number or someone not saying shit. If I didn't know any better, I would think someone was playing on my phone, but I didn't have them type of problems. "Hello?" I repeated, I could hear a baby in the background crying. And then laughter before the phone hung up. For a second, I stood wondering what was going on and if the call was made in error. Deciding to move on with my night, I continued doing what I was doing all the while shaking the funny feeling in my gut.

My Fridays entail doing me, and I mean that in the most selfish way. I'm usually at home dressed down in my favorite Tupac T-shirt- the red one with the bleach stains on the front, a pair of Ethikas, and a pair of socks that went to my knees. My scarf on my head and glasses on my face. I'd dance around my living room listening to my favorite 90's songs until I got my sixty minutes of cardio in. Friday is also my cheat day, so I like to indulge in my favorite sweet snacks and watch Lifetime until I fall asleep. But noooooo, my hot in the ass little sister is home from college for her birthday weekend. She had something planned for the entire weekend starting tonight. And, of course, I'm forced to tag along with her and Candy. So, here I am, standing in the middle of my bedroom dressed to the nines about to hang out at god only knows where. I was not fond of strip clubs, bars, nightclubs, or hood functions. I would never be caught dead at anything of the sort. Tonight, we were going to some lounge/bar, and I looked cute. I told her ass it better not be no ghetto shit and she swore to me the place is for the grown and classy.

I had on a rayon blouse with two buttons open, showing the cleavage of my D cups. I tucked my blouse into a pair of denim short shorts. My smooth thick thighs were on full display. On my feet were lime peep-toe thigh-high boots. My jet-black hair flowed underneath a black Fedora. As usual, I beat my face - gold eye shadow setting off my 3d mink lashes, and the black liner on my lower lids enhanced my chestnut-colored eyes. I lined my lips with deep red liner and filled them with nude lipstick. I loved my look. My boyfriend Blake would be pissed if he saw how I was dressed. Ever since finding out he was next to make partner in his father's law firm, he has been making snide comments about certain things that never bothered him before. Things that attracted him to me in the first place. He thought I should wear my hair in long straight weaves or pulled back into a bun. A little over two years ago, he loved how I dressed, but lately, it's been causing arguments between us. I refuse to dress up every day of the week. If it wasn't work or church, then sexy and stylish is what you'd get.

I told Toya I would meet her at the location, but she insisted that I ride in the black truck with her. Her L.A. boo was having her chauffeured around while she was here. The girl had a sponsor in every city from Cali to Florida. I tossed my cellphone, keys, mini lipstick, and gum into my lime clutch. Going into the living room, I prayed this party didn't get shot up, there were no fights or any other bullshit. I just want a fun time with my girls.

Crossing my living room, I made my way to my mini-bar and grabbed a personal bottle of Sutter Homes sweet red and took a seat on the barstool. Checking the time on my Rolex, it was a quarter to 7 pm. Toya should be pulling up any moment.

Let me introduce myself, my name is Stormy, but most call me Storm. I'm twenty-seven-years-old. I teach dance four days out of the week and work as a receptionist on Fridays and Mondays. I'm my mother's only child and the sister of my father's other children. It took some time to accept my father's other kids. First, I hated him, and secondly , he cheated on my mother to make them. Finally, about six months after I was made aware of their existence, they popped up at my graduation. They came with flowers, cards, and a plea to get to know me. We have been stuck like glue ever since. Toya adores me and I her. As far as my father, fuck him.

Blake is the love of my life. Despite our differences, he is who I will be spending the rest of my life with. I sure will be glad when I can plan my wedding. It was way overdue. His father isn't fond of him being with a black girl from the hood. Blake told his ass to accept me or lose him. I'm still on his arm at family functions.

The Facetime notification coming from my cellphone pulled me from my thoughts. I walked over to the sofa, grabbed my purse, and retrieved my cellphone from it.

"Yes," I answered. I could hear the music in the background and Candy's big mouth talking loud. Then, finally, Toya's face appeared on the screen . I smiled. She looked so pretty. Her rainbow color makeup looked good on her peanut butter skin. Her curly blonde weave adorned her oval shape face. "You look cute sister." I cooed.

"Thanks, sister. Are you ready?" she cheesed.

"Yes, here I come," I replied, grabbing my purse.

"Ok, I already got you a drink made." She said before ending the call.

As I headed toward the front door, I scanned the living room, ensuring I didn't forget anything. The moment my boot touched the entryway , my cellphone went off. It was Blake. On Fridays, we both did us. He usually didn't call until extra late.

"Hey boo," I cooed, walking toward the elevator.

"Baby, I need you to get dressed. I forgot about Michelle's birthday dinner. I am on my way." He exclaimed with urgency.

Yanking my head back, I scrunched my eyebrows in confusion.

"I am on my way out with my sister. Remember, she is here all weekend." First off, I didn't even care for

Michelle's sarcastic ass. In the short time I have known her I wanted to slap her ass a few times.

"I remember. And since she is here all weekend, she shouldn't mind you being with me tonight." I heard a door slam. It sounded like he was getting in his car.

"Blake, I can't just cancel on my sister."

"I am your man. Are you fucking your sister?" he roared. "I need you tonight, damnit. It's the least you can do."

Without giving it a second thought, I hung up on him. Shoving the phone in my purse, I decided I was done talking to Blake for the rest of the night. Sometimes he could be so damn selfish. I swear he acted like he was more important than the little family I have. I hoped he didn't call back; I didn't need my sister or cousin in my business. They already didn't care for him, they felt like he looked at them as beneath him; mainly because he always had an attitudewhenever I was with them. And if they knew of our current issue, I wouldn't hear the end of it. Before I exited my lobby, I put a smile on my face and strutted out of the building.

"Okayyyy sister, I see your sexy thick ass," Toya yelled out of the car window.

A chubby Latino guy was standing by the back door as I was approaching the black Escalade. He opened it.

Toya stepped out looking too damn cute in her black sheer bodysuit and black heels. She ran over and hugged me, squeezing me like she hadn't seen me in years. When she let me go, Candy had made her way out of the truck and hugged me also. She rocked a nude short bodysuit with clear thigh-high sandal boots, and her hair was in a high ponytail with side bangs. Candy is the light skin one out of us, and she is also loud, ruthless, and heartless . Blame that on her Uncle Moe. Toya is the wild hot in the ass dare devil. They say I'm bougie and reserved. The three of us balanced each other out. My faves drive me crazy, but I love them.

We piled back into the truck. Candy handed me a glass of dark liquor. As soon as I got it in my hand, I took a gulp. Blake and his attitude were still on my mind, but I promised myself I wouldn't let it get to me but instead enjoy my sister.

———————

"What the hell are we doing over here?" I asked Toya. We just pulled into the hood—the West Adams district, to be exact. The houses were huge but built decades ago. Most of the homes were rundown. The area itself was gang-infested—Mexicans on one side and blacks on the other. The location wasn't safe at all. I didn't understand why we were here.

"Girl, my boo wants to see me. I know he just wants to show me off to his friends. I'm with that because the nigga is going to break bread too." Toya explained, putting on her lip gloss.

"And we know you ain't coming inside. We won't be long," Candy said. She downed what was left in her glass and sat it in the cup holder.

"Carlos, let us out," Toya ordered the driver.

"I know good and damn well y'all knew I wouldn't want to come over here. You could've left me at home and came to get me after." I scolded.

"Sister, stop," Toya whined. "I swear it won't be long. I picked you up first because I didn't want you to flake on me. I know your man hates our relationship."

"It's your birthday, so I wouldn't flake, and Blake does not hate our relationship. He's just spoiled and wants me to himself."

"Yeah, we know," Candy chimed in. I cut my eyes at her.

"Y'all hurry up. I mean it. You got twenty minutes."

"K." Said my sister.

When Carlos opened the door, they climbed out. I frowned as I watched them enter the yard.

The landscaping consisted of weeds at least 3 ft tall. The paint on the house was dull and chipped. I counted at least three people standing on the porch, and they all looked like thugs. "Toya better hurry her ass up." I mumbled. I couldn't understand why the girl was attracted to such people. I busied myself with my phone. Looking up for a brief moment, I leaned closer to the window to get a better look.

"That's him," I mumbled. It was Mr. Rude. The guy from Ross's office. I knew it. I knew he had to be one of them. I could smell a drug dealer a mile away. I found myself watching his every move until he walked into the house. "Another waste of a fine black man." I shook my head knowing where the life he led would take him.

Lloyd

There was a black truck in front of the house, three knuckleheads on the porch passing blunts and talking loud. Neither saw the chicks who stepped out of the truck until they were inside the gate. The music was loud enough to hear from the street, so if the hoes were on some grimy shit and started busting, no one would be able to hear.

Across the street, ducked off in a dark blue sports car, I have been watching for the last forty-two minutes. My days of visiting the spot were over. I've walked away from the dope game. But, unfortunately, my two brothers haven't. So, I'm here, cleaning up one of their bullshit messes.

As I knew he would, Ross was able to get Julius bail. Unfortunately, because he didn't fucking listen and chose to keep the company of lame-ass people, I had to put up a half of a million to get his ass out. I don't even want to think about the stress of fighting this case if we didn't find the bitch who lied on him. My brother is innocent. I'm not saying that just because he's my sibling. Rape isn't even his character. He had plenty of hoes. Julius is cool and has a good heart, brilliant but captivated by the street life.

Two burners already on me, I slide out my ride slamming the door behind me. Eyes on the black truck wondering if anyone besides the driver was inside. Looking both ways before lightly jogging across the street, my eyes were still on the truck until I entered

47

the gate. Only two niggas were left on the porch. The other followed the bitches inside.

"What's up, OG? Oh, shit, what are you doing in our neck of the woods?" Baby Sam asked, looking around as if he was expecting someone to be with me. Probably my brothers.

I hit baby Sam with a head nod. The other little nigga I had never seen before. He gave me the once over before looking me in the eyes hitting me with a reverse nod.

"All black everything, you ain't come to play. I see you, boss."

"But y'all did. All of you little niggas out here slipping." I growled as I looked at the two. "I have been watching y'all for almost an hour. Y'all wasn't on point when the truck pulled up." I shook my head.

"We ready tho." The unknown kid said, pulling out his nine.

I hit him with a mean mug before walking into the house. The smell of weed hit me in my nose. When I got further in , I caught a whiff of one of the chick's perfume. It was the same sweet smell that ol' girl at my lawyer's office was wearing. I chuckled, thinking about how Ross said she doesn't do black men. I thought about that shit a few times. I usually didn't associate with women who didn't mess with their race, but her I wanted. If I found the time, I was going after her. Fuck her world up and leave her.

"Turn that shit off." My voice roared. And just like that, the music was off .

"If you ain't on payroll, get the fuck out," I yelled; my gaze fell on Bishop. He's the second in charge on this side.

I could see the anger in his face, but he wasn't bold enough to disobey me. He whispered into the bitch's ear he was hugged up with and then went inside his pocket, pulling out a wad. He peeled her off a few bills and placed them in her bra. She kissed him on the lips, and she and her partner headed for the door. There's that damn perfume again. I didn't even bother to look their way.

"I love me a fine as mean nigga. I see you. I am sure I will see you again." The lighter one of the two spoke. I didn't bite. She wasn't my type. She strolled out of the house. Everyone besides Bishop followed suit.

"Bishop, I'm very disappointed." I expressed. "Have a seat," I ordered, pointing to the black recliner.

Besides the dinette set in the den and the flatscreen television on the wall, it was the only piece of furniture in the fucking living room.

" I promise you I'm already on it." He stuttered. Taking a seat on the chair. "I've called J-white a few times to let them know he ain't got nothing to worry about, and that's on my mama. I'm going to handle that shit." J-white or Ghost was my youngest brother's street monikers. Real name Julius Dyce.

" What the fuck happened that night? Who is the bitch? Where does she live, and don't leave a motherfucking thing out." I growled.

"White bitch name Shelby. I met her way back in the day when she would come and cop powder. I hadn't seen her in a minute; she popped back up about a week ago. She was asking about the homies that used to be around. She came back the other day. J White pulls up. You know he ain't say shit to her. I was surprised when I told him she invited us to her party at the strip club, and he went. Her and her girls took your bro and me to a private room. The bitches were worth a couple of hundreds. I'm ready to go now. When I left out of the room, I noticed J white wasn't behind me. I'm like, nigga let's go. He put up one finger. I'm fucked up; I didn't think anything of it. I figured maybe bro wanted a second round. Or to recruit her for his shit." He shrugged. A little while later, he comes out, and as we walking out, the police swoop up on us, and the bitch pointed our way, screaming rape. I thought we both were gone, but her focus was on my boy. You know I wasn't going to let that shit ride. I waited for the hoe, but she got picked up by some old-ass white lady. I had the home girl follow her. Bitch ain't getting away with whatever weird shit she on."

"Sounds like a setup." I gave him a warning look.

"Either that or the bitch was doped up out of her mind. Something but I'm on whatever you on."

I didn't need him. I could handle the shit myself. He gave me her address, and I prepared to leave. I took two steps....

Boka Boka Boka… gun shots rang out. I dropped to the floor, pulling my gun from my waistband. Glass shattered and bullets whizzed past my head. Fear didn't even cross my mind; I was angry as fuck. I hated to think a mutha fucka was bold enough to come for me or anyone I associate with. As I impatiently waited for my chance to bust back, I thought about who was trying to send a message because that is definitely what was going on. Once the shots let up, Bishop and I ran outside. My eyes landed on Baby Sam laid out on the ground with a bullet to his head. Everyone else was lying on their stomachs, panicking.

"Who were the bitches?"

"Toya, my college boo. She ain't on that type of shit." I gave him a hard stare. He shook his head, "Trust me." I gawked at him a few seconds more before my eyes fell back on Baby Sam.

"Handle it." I jogged off the porch to my ride. Sirens could be heard when I got up the block. Grabbing my other phone from my console, I called a good friend to make sure the officers they sent to the scene would only be concerned about who was shooting and nothing more. Next stop, Shelby's spot.

Stormy

Blake: *It never fails, every time you are around them you forget I am the man who loves you. Don't call me, I will call you.*

My nose flared while reading the text. Every chance he got he wanted me to feel bad. I shoved my phone back into my purse. Blake knew what I had planned, and I refused to feel bad this time. He should've told me about the party ahead of time. My eyes landed across the table. Candy was so pretty; it was sad that she refused to love. She has never been hurt by a man. The girl had an icebox where her heart is supposed to be.

"Woman, what are you over there thinking about?" I asked Candy.

She sat across from me, sipping on a margarita while staring into a daze. Toya was sitting next to her, eating a Cesar salad.

After leaving that trap spot, we came to have dinner at Toya's favorite steak house. DB Prime Steak. It's my first time at the establishment, in fact, my first time hearing of it. It wasn't what I was expecting. Not fancy at all but doable. The location was excellent, located in the heart of downtown Long Beach. You could see the ocean up the block from where we were sitting. The building was twice as big as a coffee shop. When we pulled up to the valet, Toya informed me the restaurant was black-owned. My sister loved a good meal and could cook. I knew for a fact the place had to serve delicious food. I couldn't wait. Everything on the menu seemed appealing.

"Ok, this bitch been in a daze since we got here." Toya chimed in, giggling, looking at Candy.

"Girl, I'm thinking about the dude that walked in that trap house. Rude. Fine, and those eyes. I would fuck him more than once." She pursed her lips.

I damn near choked on the biscuit I was eating. It wasn't what Candy said that got me, it was who she was talking about. If I told them how he tried to flirt with me at the office today, Toya's ass would make it her business to hook me up.

"What fine man?" I asked, trying to play it off.

"The one that checked Toya's boo." She retorted, looking at Toya. "Had that nigga looking like a straight pussy." She shook her head.

"Storm, but if you would've seen that fine ass nigga, I think you would've wanted him for yourself." Candy insinuated. "Tall, athletic build, whisky complexion. Full juicy lips, dark grey eyes, and thick eyebrows. I don't even like dreads but baby ." She licked her lips, "Damn, he was fine, with his mean ass. He looked like he was one of those hood legends too."

I continued to eat my biscuit as if I wasn't listening. But I knew exactly who she was talking about.

"First of all," Toya started, "he didn't check nobody. So don't do my boo." She playfully rolled her eyes while pointing her fork at Candy.

"He did more than check him. He made him look weak. Don't talk to him anymore. He can't protect you."

"Go to hell." Toya laughed. "As long as he got money for me when I ask, I don't care how scary he is."

"I know that's right." Candy agreed, they high fived each other.

We continued to talk and crack jokes. Thoughts of Mr. Rude invaded my mind. I tried to picture him and Candy as a couple, but I was not too fond of it. Shifting my thoughts to Blake, I was wondering how long he would stay mad at me. Maybe I should have gone to the party.

"Good evening, ladies." A deep voice caused all of us to look up from the table. Standing before us was a dark skin guy with cognac-colored eyes and a friendly white smile. I noticed the notepad and pen in his hand and furrowed my eyebrows. I figured it couldn't be the waiter dressed like that. He was dressed in a red Polo shirt with a name tag that read Boss. Dark blue jeans and wheat Timberlands on his feet. A red Cincinnati baseball cap covered his bald head. You couldn't miss the diamond watch on his wrist and the two thick chains around his neck. The more I stared at him the more he looked like someone I knew. It was the eyebrows and thick lips that seemed familiar.

"Hello." Toya returned the greeting.

"What happened to our waiter?" Candy inquired, giving him a once over before staring in his eyes as if she was challenging him; it was her way of flirting. She should've been a boy the way she handles dudes.

"Don't worry. I'll take care of you." Boss eyed Candy like she was a steak, licking his lips and all.

"Can you take our order before you come over here flirting?" Toya chimed in. "We are hungry. Plus, we are on a schedule."

"You got that." Then, he looked at Candy, "what's your name?"

"Candy," she replied. "Why do they call you Boss?"

"For many reasons." He smirked. "What you trying to eat, baby?"

"Excuse you?" I exclaimed, "you know that isn't professional, the way you're acting."

He looked at me like I was bothering him,

"Stop being rude. I'm trying to take the beautiful lady's order." He said before giving his attention back to Candy. "Now, what are you having?"

Candy ordered a steak well done. I shook my head. I never understood why people ordered their steak that way. Toya ordered salmon, and I had the same. We requested mashed potatoes, lobster mac, green beans, and spinach for the sides.

"Alright. I'm going to put your order in. Since you ladies are so beautiful, and I made your girl mad." He looked at me, and I rolled my eyes, "everything is one me."

"Awww, thanks, and it's my birthday," Toya cooed.

"Happy birthday. Enjoy."

"Thank you." She replied, taking the last gulp of her drink.

"I need another drink," Toya said.

"I'll send someone over. I'm about to head out." He looked at Candy, " I need your number. I'm going to take you out Sunday."

" I never said I was single or interested. Thanks for dinner, but it ain't worth my pussy." She stated matter of factly.

I gasped, looking around, hoping no one heard her. And Boss, he just stood there laughing like it was the funniest thing he ever heard.

"Woman, put your number in my phone. I gotta go. He handed her his cell. Candy reluctantly took the cell from his hand and punched her number in.

"If you don't call on Sunday, don't even bother. I mean it." Candy tossed.

"Woman cut it out. You just better answer. You ladies enjoy your night," he turned to walk off,

"Aye, Boss," Toya called out.

Just a few steps away, he stopped and turned around.

"What's up, birthday girl!"

"You wouldn't happen to have a mean brother, same eyes as yours, would you?"

Then, with a smile, he stared at her.

"Do you?" I found myself asking.

"It depends on why you are asking." He looked from me to Toya.

Toya shrugged, "no big deal, you just favored someone Candy thought was fine." He looked at Candy with raised brows.

"Don't let your girls get you in trouble. May as well tell your boy toys, Boss will have all your time." He gave her a knowing look and walked off.

"Looks like someone met their match." Toya teased.

Candy smiled. " I ain't thinking about his hoe ass, " she lied. We watched as Boss took off running out of the restaurant.

By the time we left the restaurant, we were stuffed and tipsy. I sure wanted to take a raincheck on the lounge, but I knew better- Toya would have a fit.

As we grabbed our things, Toya called herself trying to boss me around.

"I'm not playing, you better get up and dance. You claim dance is your life but never showcase your talent." Toya fussed.

"Right, y'all heffas got all the moves. I bet you won't catch my two-stepping ass sitting down." Candy cut in. "Stop being a prude, dance, have fun- live."

"I do dance and have fun, and I live." I snapped. "Just because I don't dance in clubs or freak on any fine man who wants a dance don't mean I ain't having a good time."

"You better dance tonight is all I know," Toya warned.

"Excuse me." I offered, bumping into a lady dressed in a black two-piece pants suit.

"You are excused." She snapped, giving me the once over.

My head jerked back. With my face frowned up I stared in disbelief. It had been damn near eleven years, but I would never forget the blue eyed red head slut. I looked at Candy, she was staring at the chick with a smirk.

"That's the bitch you knocked in the mouth back in the day." Candy said, taking a couple of steps closer to the chick. "She still ain't learned, keep it up and you will find yourself back on the ground." Candy warned.

"Yeah, bitch." Toya sassed, ready to show her ass.

"I bet you ghetto trash will be in jail if you touch me." She threatened.

Gawking, I thought about how she called me a weak bitch that night at the party. That stung. I wanted to knock her in the mouth again. Fighting never solved anything.

"Come on y'all." I said walking off, "she ain't worth it. One day somebody is going to knock her teeth out."

As Candy and Toya trailed behind me, they called her all kinds of names. The driver had the back door open; I couldn't climb in fast enough.

Seeing her made me think of Deon and how he dissed me at the party that night. My stomach balled up in knots. I tried to block out the part about me walking in and finding my mother dead, but it was hard. When I felt my eyes burning, I hurried and made myself a drink taking it to the head.

"Let's party and I promise I am dancing." I declared. Both Candy and Toya hugged me.

"Carlos turn that shit up." Toya ordered the driver, and we started singing Solider by Destiny's Child.

Julius

Sunday

I was down for almost 72 hours all because a bitch wanted to lie on me. Everyone in L.A. knew I didn't have to rape nobody. What ol' girl was on was going to be the cause of her demise. If she thought she would get away with the bullshit she was stupid as fuck.

Shrugging my shoulders, I head out my hotel room. I am far from worried about what the outcome would be-this shit was going to disappear. My brothers and the homies been calling me but I haven't answered. Like, I said, I needed to clear my head.

Thirty minutes later, I pulled up to our trap in the low bottoms. There was yellow tape around the gate and the porch letting me know it was a crime scene. One narc car and a black and white sat out front. I'm glad the Tommy Hawk I was driving was rented. I didn't need my license plate ran for shit. If. You. don't know J-White -At first glance, you'll look at me and think I'm this geeky ass white boy but if you are a thinker, you would wonder what a dude like me was doing making the moves I be making, hanging with the niggas I be with and playing with the hoes I choose. I'm a Florida boy but Cali is home too. It's where I'm comfortable being me. Put it like this, I'm a Gemini which means I am two people. You'll learn more about me later tho.

Needing to find out what was going down I headed straight to the club. We didn't do no talking over the phone. On my way over I used my burner phone to hit up Bishop.

"What up bro?" I greeted B. He was with me that night.

"J-White, you out? Man, I'm coming to you." He said, sounding frustrated and happy to hear from me at the same time.

"The club. Northridge." Was all I said, before hanging up.

The strip club I owned with my brother was in the valley about forty minutes away. I got there in thirty. Only a few cars were in the parking lot of the black and gold brick building. On Sunday, Monday & Tuesday's we did all day Happy Hour. It was a little after noon, the crowd didn't fall through until after two. I parked in my reserved spot and pulled out my burner calling up my oldest brother. I didn't feel like dealing with his bossy, I'll fix everything, focus on school ass. Niggas get old and forget they once enjoyed the same life I'm living. I don't know if he was mad or tore up but after hitting him twice and getting no answer I was done calling. I then hit up Boss.

"Speak," he greeted.

"It's me," I replied.

"Good to hear your voice. I'm in the middle of something but I'll get with you ASAP!"

I gave a reverse nod as if he could see me. Two things I figured. Lloyd & him already handled or was in the process of handling our current issues. Ross told me how Lloyd came up to his office tripping. I can almost bet he hit up Bishop.

Tossing the phone in the glovebox I climbed out my ride. The warm sun beaming down on my skin put me in the mood to go surfing. I made a mental note to go to the beach when I got back to Florida. I didn't have class on Tuesday, so I'd go then.

Before entering my establishment, I greeted my security guard. He told me he heard about what happened and to let him know if I needed anything. One thing about the Dyce brothers- we get major love out in the streets but for the most part, we handle our own affairs.

"Good looking," I said, strolling into the club.

Just that quick it went from a warm sunny day to a cool dark night. R&B played as dancers walked around greeting our guests. When my bartender's eyes landed on me she smiled big. She finished servicing her customer before running over and giving me a hug.

"We heard what happened." Lala said, putting a hand on her hip. She was a cute dark skin girl with a fat ass. Lala was married but wanted me bad. I was cool. Plus, I really didn't care for my women to be too seasoned. Old ladies wasn't my thang.

"What's up J-White?" A stripper by the name of Zion spoke.

"Why you ain't on stage?"

"I got another twenty minutes. I'm about to do a few lap dances. Let me know if you want me and the crew to go handle them bitches at Paradise. We don't play about you." She said.

I smirked.

"I will let you know." I hit her on the ass making a smacking sound and her crazy ass began to make it clap.

"See you later boo. I swear, you give me a chance, you won't regret it."

"Girl, you and me both." Lala chimed in, glaring at my dick. I peeped the salty look Zion gave her. If she wasn't my employee, I would take her down.

"Y'all burnt."

"Shiiid, I had me a white boy before. Not only was the dick good but I ain't never had to pay a bill for the five years I was with him. Damn. I wish he didn't die." Lala said, shaking her head.

"He must've been old." Zion spat. She looked at me. "I bet them college girls ain't doing it like you need." She switched off. Damn, calm down boy.

I smirked. Instantly thought of this one chick in my history class. Fine, body bad, and knew how to work a pole. I wanted her bad but for my sanity I deemed her off limits.

"Can your boy get a drink?" I said to Lala.

"Yes." She replied.

I turned around and looked toward the door to see what Lala was looking at. It was Bishop. Time to handle business.

Stormy

Monday

Sitting up in my king-size bed, I stretched while yawning. I slept like a baby; between the rain and all the partying I did over the weekend I was exhausted. Before rising from the bed, I looked over at my cellphone sitting on my nightstand. Picking it up, I ended the alarm. Next, I checked the texts and call log. Blake's ass hadn't called since Friday, and I was pissed. I was going to give him until the end of the day. He's always acting like a brat when he can't get his way. It irked me.

Stepping down onto the plush carpet, I stretched again, touching my toes, and twisting from side to side. I took my tan suit out last night. I was showered, dressed, and headed out the door with my smoothie in hand within an hour.

As I pulled out of the parking structure, ready to blast my favorite CD, my cellphone rang. Hitting decline, I rolled my eyes at my father's name on the screen. I didn't feel like dealing with his shit today. Like I said, I don't fuck with him.

It took me thirty minutes to make it to the job. When I walked into the office, I was shocked by the beautiful display that was on my desk.

"Oh my god." I cooed, rushing over. I sat my things behind my desk. I picked up the vase full of black and blue roses and smelled them. My heart fluttered. Blake can be an asshole one minute, and Prince Charming the next.

"Good morning Mr. Ross." I greeted, putting the vase back on my desk.

"Good morning." He replied, walking out of the door.

Grabbing the card and reading it, I blushed. *"You are mine. Enjoy your day, beautiful."* It was the simple things. I called Blake to thank him, but he didn't answer. So instead, I sent a text; I love you and thank you.

Mr. Ross walked back into the office with a smile on his face sipping from his coffee.

"I see you like your roses. Those things are expensive. They last a year, you know."

"I didn't," I said, touching them.

"So, are you going to go on a date with him?" he asked. Taking another sip from his coffee, he sat in a chair in the lobby crossing his legs.

"A date with who?" I inquired.

"My client? Lloyd Dyce."

"No, I have a man and who's your client. Dyce?"

"The rude ass gentleman that got you the thousand-dollar roses." He stood up.

Now, I'm confused. "Who?"

"Lloyd Dyce. The asshole who barreled into the office last week. He delivered them himself."

My mouth dropped. Mr. Ross stood in place for a moment .

"I think you should go on a date with him. My godson ain't shit but a spoiled prick anyway. I won't tell him if you don't." Then, shaking his head, he made his way up the stairs.

I don't know what the hell Ross and Lloyd Dyce had going on, but they needed to leave me out of it. I wanted so badly to call Toya and Candy and tell them that the mean guy who punked Toya's dude and who Candy wanted to fuck sent me roses. I was smarter than that tho. They would go out of their way to get us together. They hated Blake but he wasn't even that bad. I believe deep down it's because he is white. I love him, and that is all that matters.

Toya

Back in Florida

"Why are you handling me like a trick, Ma?" LD scoffed. I didn't give a damn about him being mad. He knew the rules; you have a pay to play. My momma taught me that. LD is a dude I met at the club. Cute, peanut butter complexion with gold locks. He stood about six feet with a body of a god. He's the type of nigga that can get a bitch wet just by looking at his sexy ass. His tiny dick would probably make a bitch mad when she gave it up, not me tho. Little Dick can hit this all he wants as long as he pays. LD always broke bread: hence, I'm with him tonight. But he is giving me broke nigga vibes right now. I ain't with that.

"No money, no pussy." I said with my hand out, "as a matter of fact, I'm gone," I grabbed my purse off the small table in our tiny ass motel room. "I shouldn't even have come up." I turned around to face him, pissed the fuck off that he was trying to play me. Pointing my pink acrylic nail in his face, I said, " make this your last time playing with me. You cute and all, but I don't play about my money." I then mushed him in the head.

"That's fucked up," he grabbed me by the arm, pulling me back toward him. "I have been fucking you for a few months. I give you more than I give my baby momma."

"And what the fuck does that mean?" I looked at him from his black and white sneakers to his face. The Starburst edibles I ate, and his dumb-ass comment had the nigga looking real goofy to me; shit was comical I had to laugh. "If your baby momma doesn't know her worth that's on that bitch." I snatched my hand from him, pointing at my chest, "Toya knows her worth. I ain't only fine, but I'm smart and what's between my legs," I placed my hand between my legs rubbing my pussy, "is more precious than jewels."

One thing about me, the only man's pockets I give a fuck about is my daddy's. My brothers know not to ask me for much. They give to me and always have... I don't really give a damn about the next woman nor her pockets, but I'm human, and sometimes I wonder why in the fuck they are so caught up on being their nigga's ride or die. Like, what type of crown do they get because they are holding their nigga down? Bitch will he do it for you? My pussy and time aren't free unless I want to fuck with you like that and that rarely was the case. I gotta get something out of the deal. Women are dumb over dick but not me.

"Your shit is a jewel. I respect your hustle." I watched as he went into his pocket. Little baby pulled out a wad. I counted $300.00, and when he held it out to to me, I placed my hand on my hip.

"Nigga an extra hundred will be nice since you wanna play."

"You tried it. Take it or leave it."

I snatched the money quickly and put it in my purse.

Now, all smiles, I tossed the purse back on the table and peeled my clothes off. I didn't have any more time to waste. My roommate wanted to link, and I haven't seen the hoe in weeks. Her little girlfriend kept her tucked away at her place. She already told me she thought we had something going on. I was the last person she should've thought wanted her woman; I don't do fish.

"Got damn." He shouted, eyeing my body. I turned around in a circle so he could take me all In.

"That red looks good. " He referred to my red lace G. I was too messy, never cared for bras. "Take that shit off," I ordered, stepping back watching with lust. All I could think about was him sucking on my pussy. That was a must, no matter if they were paying upfront or thought they were breaking their little boo thang off.

LD undressed in records time. I kept my eyes on every part of his body except the dick. That little pink thang was a turn-off. Caressing his muscler body, I growled like a lion.

"Come on, make me cum right quick." I pulled him by the arm and fell back on the bed. He stood between my legs, eyeing my pussy.

"Arrrggggh," his growl was much louder and more aggressive than mine. Finally, LD dropped to his knees, took my panties off with his teeth, and ate my pussy until I came.

"Got damn," I exclaimed. He smiled as he slid on the condom he retrieved from the pocket of his jeans. Then, climbing on top of me, he guided himself into my dripping wet box.

"Awww, just like that." I moaned. Two hours later, I was out.

———————

"Which one of you ugly broke tramp ass bitches stole my shit?" I yelled, slamming the locker and turning to face the throwback ass bitches who swore they were strippers.

The twins continued to dress for their set. The new hoe who wanted to come to work and make friends so bad looked at me through the mirror as she continued to brush her dry ass weave. Then there was the old bitch, Diamond with a foot on the bench putting lotion on her spotted ass legs while she talked to her flunky, a bitch name Suppa.

"We don't move like that, Desire." One of the twins replied as they headed out of the locker room.

The other added, "on the dead homies, if we knew, we wouldn't say shit. Ain't no snitching over here." They strutted out the door.

"On my momma, you hoes done fucked up. I bet your broke ass stole it, Diamond." I yelled. I was pissed.

"And if I did, you ain't going to do shit." Diamond challenged, still rubbing lotion on her frog legs.

I gave that bitch a death stare. In my opinion, she was telling me she had my shit. Deep down, I believe that she did. I wanted to whoop her ass, but I wasn't trying to get jumped. All I wanted to do was come to work and make money. I had someone depending on me. Miserable bitches with no life goals, or morals, refused to let a go-getter be great.

I'd just made it to work. I threw my duffle bag and purse into my locker and rushed off to the bathroom. I walked back into the locker room, discovering my got damn purse was gone. And the bitches had the nerve to leave my cellphone on top of my bag

"You right, I ain't going to do shit." I retorted with a chuckle, grabbing my duffle bag.

"So, stop all that pump faking like you with the shits." Suppa instigated.

"You can have all that shit in my purse. It's all replaceable. Including the punk-ass five hundred in there. With or without the wallet, I am still going to be smarter, cuter, sexier, and always make more money than you." I stared back and forth between Diamond and Suppa. Bitches looked like they were rejects from one of the worst projects in Florida. Ol' dirty country hoes.

"Keep talking, and you are going to get fucked up." Diamond barked.

"Diamond, I ain't about to fight you. I am too cute for that. I am done with this wack -ass club." I declared . "Wherever I go, I will still make more money than you."

They both laughed. I gave a reverse nod as I glared at them, envisioning the satisfaction I would have when I got revenge on they asses . Before I made my exit, I looked at the weakest link, still brushing her weave.

"Stop trying to fit in. That shit is lame." I walked out with my head held high. Them bitches couldn't stop me if they wanted to.

———

"What the fuck, dude," I yelled, looking at the four flat tires on my red Lexus.

Tears immediately ran down my face. I didn't have my wallet so, I couldn't call AAA, and I didn't even want to wait on them. I just wanted to get away as fast as possible from this club. My roommate was at a party with her chick. I didn't feel like dealing with the two niggas I mess with out here. I was stuck. I started walking. I didn't stop until I was a good distance away from the club. It was dark on these Florida roads. I'm from the hood, but this down south shit wasn't something I was used to. I believed they still hung black folks out here.

Pulling my phone out, I called my friend. It was after eleven. I knew his nerd ass wasn't gone anywhere. I only hoped he wasn't asleep. Ju did turn in early.

"Yo." He said in a groggy voice, trying to sound like he was hip. I smiled because I knew he was only acting like that because I was calling. Ju had a crush on me. I bet when he saw my name his eyes lit up.

Ju is a guy from school I study with from time to time. We kicked it off campus a few times too. He never tried to make a pass at me, but I knew he had a big crush on me. I don't do nerds or white boys, and he's both.

"Ju, can you come to pick me up? I have a flat tire. More like four." I whined, calling him by the nickname I gave him. He claimed he hated it, but he still answered to it. His government is Julius. Now, you see why I like to call him Ju.

"Stop calling me that, Toya; I am sleeping. Call AAA or something." He grunted. "Call one of them dudes who face you stay in."

I looked at the phone, not appreciating how he snapped at me—putting it on speaker because I had something to say I snaked my neck.

"What do you mean call AAA?"

"I said I am sleeping."

"Nigga, you should be happy to pick me up. If someone sees you rolling around with a bad bitch like me, it may get you some pussy. Shit." I snapped, rolling my eyes. "You got me twisted. Do you know who I am?"

When I didn't get a response, I looked at my phone and saw my screen saver. Ju's ass hung up on me. Immediately I called him back, and he sent me to voicemail. My phone vibrated, and I saw that he had sent me a text.

Ju: Don't call me no more asking for favors. Females like you come a dime a dozen, and I ain't interested. Be safe.

No, the fuck he didn't. Everybody wanted to try me tonight. I wanted to call Stormy and Toya so bad, but they would question my reason for being out so late. They didn't know I still danced.

Lloyd

"Good morning." I greeted my brothers when I entered the enormous kitchen. A flood of emotions came rushing over me; old memories and wishing my parents were still here. This is the home we grew up in. The kitchen was my mother's favorite part of the house. She was a good cook and taught Boss to be one as well. When they died, Julius decided to move out of his apartment and back home.

"Good morning," they replied in unison.

Julius was sitting at the kitchen table with his laptop in his face, and Boss was standing over the stove doing what he did best; whip up something good for us to eat. I smirked, watching him smile at whoever he was bullshitting with on the phone.

"When I get back in town, I'm going to kidnap your little ass. Lock you up until you get some act right." Boss said into the phone. You couldn't take that nigga and women serious for shit. He was a big ass player.

Pulling out a chair across from baby bro, I grabbed the cup of orange juice from in front of him and took a gulp. Staring at Julius, my heart swelled. I was proud of him but at the same time worried. At twenty-three, he was already one year away from attending medical school. If my nigga made it to see thirty, he would get that white coat—officially become a doctor. I pray that he would walk away from the game then.

Julius, aka J-White, aka Ghost, is a gangster. Didn't take any shit; he was quick to pull the trigger or make a mutha fucka suffer depending on his mood. Niggas in our city knew not to fuck with him. Baby bro could handle his own, but my concern was when he's home in Cali, he is reckless in the streets. Hence, the rape charge. I hoped to have disappeared before court. But, if Shelby didn't get the message sent, it would be her head cut off next.

"The food is almost done," Boss announced.

"It better be good too." I teased.

" I'm cooking for my brothers," Boss explained to whoever was on the phone. Me and Ju looked at each other. Since when did he start explaining himself? "See, now you got these niggas looking at me like I am a simp or something. My brothers know I do not explain myself to nobody."

I shook my head. Ju went back to typing on his MAC.

"What's bothering you?" I questioned. I could see the annoyance on his face.

Letting out a hard breath, he reached for his glass of orange juice.

"Man," he whined, grabbing the jug from the center of the table and pouring himself more.

"So, what's the problem? Is it the case?" I asked.

He shook his head no. Then, pushing his black frames up on his face, he looked at me.

"If she becomes a problem, then I will off everyone close to her, make that bitch lose her mind, and wait for her to kill herself ." His tone was so cold it almost had me shivering. Baby bro wasn't to be fucked with.

"Let me handle that; you worry about school. She has already been warned." I told him, staring at him in the eyes. He grimaced.

I know he didn't like my response; he felt like I treated him like a baby. I only wanted what was best for him. The street life wasn't it.

"Anyway." Julius started. "It's this chick."

"AYE, LET ME CALL YOU BACK, MY LITTLE BROTHER GOT CHICK ISSUES," Boss yelled on the phone and laughed.

"What's up?" I urged him to continue, ignoring Boss.

"She called me last night talking crazy. Telling me I better be happy that she even allows me to be next to her or some shit like that." He frowned.

"And what you tell the hoe?" Boss asked, setting our plates of Shrimp and Grits in front of us.

"I hung up on her. I ain't wanna cuss her silly ass out."

"Because you like her, huh?" I asked with a grin.

"I did, but the last few months, I don't know." He slumped in his chair.

"How long have you liked her?" Boss asked.

"About a year. Well, I've had a crush on her, but I started liking her about six months now."

"You ain't step to her?" I questioned. Bro wasn't scared to talk to chicks.

"She likes hood niggas. I low-key think she is a gold digger. She's the true definition of taking the girl out of the hood, but you can't take the hood out of the girl. She's from Cali too. I think Inglewood. Surprise I haven't seen her around."

"Why did you stop liking her or feel like you wanna fall back?" I probed.

"Apart from the niggas I have seen her with, I can tell she doesn't know her worth. And if she ain't feeling me for who I am, then I'm cool. I don't like that shit she was talking last night either."

I gave him a nod. I understood and respected it.

"Bro, you got the best of both worlds. You like her. She wants a thug. Show her you can be that too." Boss added his two cents.

My eyes darted toward Boss; the nigga said the most stupid shit at times.

"She gets what I present. I fuck with Toya because she is cool and from what she showed, real. Plus, she's fine and her body is banging. She's a stripper, too. She couldn't be my girl and dance, but I respect her hustle. The broad came at me sideways. I probably would've yoked her ass up if she was in my face." He looked at me, " tired of mutha fuckas thinking I'm some lame as a white boy."

"But you are a nerdy ass white boy with the heart of a lion. You are a giver. Handsome. Money is long. If she is for you, it'll work out." I advised.

" Stop gassing his ass up, he over here turning red and shit, but it's true," Boss added. "She doesn't deserve you. I can bet she doesn't."

We sat in silence for a minute, all in our thoughts. I was thinking about the flowers I sent to Ross's receptionist and how she ain't called to say thank you. I know Ross gold her they were from me, he said he even left my number on her desk. If the woman thought she would play me to the left, she thought wrong. Stormy was all up in my head.

"Aye, I got this chick I wanna push up on. She is black, but Ross says she doesn't fuck with black men. So, you know that's a challenge for me, right?" I looked at both my brothers.

"Here you go." Julius laughed.

"How the fuck she black and don't mess with niggas? I can't stand them kind of bitches." Boss scoffed .

"I am going to make her regret her words," I assured them.

"Is she fine, nice ass?" Boss asked with a raised brow.

"You already know. "

"Do it, bro." Ju urged me and winked.

We sat in silence for a while as we ate. I appreciated having normal

conversations with my brothers. For the most part, we got along well. We weren't jealous of one another and shared almost everything that was going on in our lives with each other. I say almost because humans didn't share everything. My only complaint about my bros was that they did not want to walk away from the family hustle. They would say their issue with me was that I want to be the boss. I'm the oldest, so that's how it goes.

"I met this little hoe at the restaurant; she came in with her girls. She playing hard to get, remind me of me, but I'm going to break her little ass ." Boss shared.

We laughed at Boss's comment. But I could tell Julius was still bothered. It had me wondering if he more than likes this girl.

We finished our food, and I decided to wash the dishes. Today made a year since we lost our parents, and we were going to their gravesites. That's why Boss and I were down in Florida.

————————

Johana & Johnny Dyce. I could never take anything from the legendary Bonnie and Clyde. But I must say my mother and father were just as ruthless and dangerous. Born and raised in the UK, they got it out of the mud young. Home invasions, scamming, and bank robbery were just a few crimes they committed. It wasn't until they came up on a drug lick that they fled to Florida. The states may have hated them, but my brother Boss, born Jordon & I would be forever grateful.

Two adolescents, five and eight, left for days in an abandoned house by our mother. When the couple ran into the house to flee from some niggas they got over on, it was the best day of our life.

We were two hungry black kids in soiled clothes, and   rat bites. The Dyce's made sure we never remembered our tarnished childhood. That night they took us in, and we didn't protest. They raised us as their own and trained us to be just like them— dangerous cold-hearted hustlers. It's a story to be told. A homey-looking white couple was raising two ghetto black boys. Looking at them, you would never know they were the plug. All the rules of the game we were taught by them.

Eight years later, our parents gave birth to Julius. We all were ordered to be college graduates. Couldn't be no dumb criminals. Momma wanted Ju to become a doctor. The degree would be an asset to our family hustle. Boss has a degree in Criminal Justice and me, accounting.

We supplied every hustler from Cali to the south and even the UK. Whether it was pills or crack we supplied it. Boss and I were ordered to leave Florida and run southern Cali when I was 18. We both checked into USC. While in the dope game, I graduated with my master's and Boss a few years later. Life was good. Money, whatever chick we desired, and more.

Our parents were on a road trip a year ago, and their car went over a cliff. Fucked us all up. Right after the funeral, I made my exit from the game. I felt too much of anything would be a man's downfall. In actuality, none of us needed the money. More so, power and because that's what Dyce's are.

"We miss y'all," Boss said, looking at the grave. He took it the hardest. He was a momma's boy. He and mom had a tight relationship.

"A lot," I added; we all missed them.

Julius used the back of his hand to wipe a tear from his eye. We stood there in our thoughts. I thought about the promise I made to my father before he passed. Desperately I wanted to tell him the deal was off, but I couldn't do it. Even afterlife, I was loyal to those loyal to me.

Deon

I was anxiously sitting in my cell waiting for the punk ass police to finish the count; I needed to make a phone call to my boys on the outside. Finally, after seven years, I could taste the free world in exactly two weeks . I couldn't wait to get up out of this bitch. But most importantly, I couldn't wait to take my spot back in the game. Our crew could no longer hold it down without me, and Naz was gone. While a few of the homies tried to stay afloat by pushing nickels and dimes, a lot of them niggas like Bishop went to the other side. Niggas forgot where they came from and who fed them when they didn't have shit. Not once did Bishop try to lookout. All he cared about was himself. We have never been as close as Naz and me, but he was part of the team, and because of that, he was considered family. Family lookout for family. And since he never looked out, he was now an OPP.

I looked down at my watch, already thinking about how I was about to do a major upgrade in just a matter of weeks and get me a Cartier and some fly ass gear. My heart swelled, knowing I was about to get my life back. I am the Queen's son; a nigga is royalty, and royalty lives the lavish life by any means necessary.

Jumping up from my bunk, I looked out the cell and could see the coast was clear. Climbing back on the bed, I laid back and dialed the homie's number, put the burner phone to my ear, and waited for him to answer .

"What's up, my boy?" I said. He answered on the first ring.

" Man, a whole lot." Detecting the frustration in his tone I already knew it was some shit.

" Talk mutha fucka, What's up?" I roared.

" We went by there and lit that mutha fucka up. So far I ain't heard if we hit nobody but trust me, we sent a mutha fucking message."

"Good. So, what's the problem?"

"I just got a call from Shelby; she scared as shit. Say somebody broke into her house and left a dozen of dead rats, and the mutha fucking heads were

chopped off. Somebody trying to send her a message, and she's scared for her and the baby."

"Word?" I responded, not really giving a fuck. Her punk-ass daddy is the reason I'm in here. Bitch nigga got mad because I was fucking his daughter. I thought nothing of it; what the fuck was he going to do to me? Had the bitch told me she was the daughter of a cop, I probably would've stopped fucking with her. I ain't find out shit until me and Naz were pulled over and arrested for two bricks. The nigga was the one who read me my rights. I wanted to kill that bitch. Then she turned around and had a baby by me like that meant something. Fuck her and that baby. He's six.

"You still there?"

"Yeah," I answered.

"But peep this. You sent her on Bishop. He ain't the one they arrested. They gaffled up a white boy. Word on the street is he's Bishop's connect. But the nigga they showed me, I don't know. And why would the connect hang with his worker?"

"Find out. You never know."

"You know I'm on it.

What about Shelby?" he asked.

"What about her ? All that other shit ain't my problem. Find out about the white boy. Get ready; we about to take over. Keep hitting them niggas."

"Bet. I pick Naz up tomorrow."

I told him to call me. Thanks to the deals we took, we both were coming home around the same time. They ain't ready.

I hid the phone in my jar of peanut butter. Then, rising from the bed, I shook my celli.

"Nigga get up." I ordered, stroking my dick.

"I'm sleeping." He mumbled. The slap to his face woke his ass up. I didn't give a fuck about him getting mad.

"Hurry up," I ordered; he jumped from the bed, dropped to his knees, and took me into his warm mouth, slurping and sucking like a pro. Within three minutes, he was swallowing my seeds.

" Check your books tomorrow." I informed him. I took care of mine.

Toya

One week later

"Oh my god, that was so fun," I said to Jeremiah. We'd just pulled up to the Firehouse. He rode me on the back of his sports bike. I swear I have always been scared to ride a motorcycle, but somehow, I let this fine-ass brother convince me that it was safe and fun. I'm glad that I did. A warm Friday night dressed in short white shorts, a T-shirt representing my university, and black and white J's. My long silk weave blew underneath my helmet as Jeremiah sped through Tampa.

"Let me teach you how to ride, get you a bike and apply to join our crew. We need pretty girls like you."

I blushed, handing him my helmet. The man had game. I knew cap when I heard it, and depending on the nigga's pockets or how fine they were, I let them run it on me thick while I ate that shit up.

Jeremiah was from a popular bike club and was fine; chicks flocked to him like dope heads to a dealer. It didn't make any difference to me because I wasn't interested. Money wasn't long enough, and you could tell he wanted to be hard. He wasn't about that life. Tonight, he caught me at the right time. I was bored between looking for another club to try out and just needing some air. I had just left out of the library when he stepped to me.

"You so damn fine. All I want to do is take you out for a good time. I know you out of my league ." He placed his hand on his chest, "but baby, if you'll please let me feed you some wings and you pretend like you like my company in front of my boys, I'll owe you my life."

I laughed so hard—his pick-up line was cute and corny. I said yes.

The parking lot was deep with bikers, a few people from car clubs, thots, regular people; you name it. On Friday's Firehouse was always popping.

Jeremiah introduced me to a couple of his friends. He fired up a blunt and asked me if I smoked. I shook my head no, "but I drink," I said.

"Give me a minute. I'm 'bout to get you something." He strolled off. He went over to a guy standing by a blue sports bike and whispered something in his ear. The guy reached inside the cooler next to him and handed him two bottles. I smiled as he walked back over with a pint of Hennessy and a 5th of Grey goose.

"Pick your poison, baby, whatever you want."

"Thank you," I replied, taking the Grey goose bottle from him.

"I need a cup."

"Gotchu," he said. Before he could even turn around, some female walked up and offered him a cup.

"I know you don't like hot liquor." She told him, shaking the ice around in the cup.

"I ain't drinking. I'm going to give it to her."

She smiled facedly, looked at me, and then back at Jeremiah.

I just didn't trust bitches. There was always some kind of hate. Jealous of the next bitch. Being that Jeremiah was fine and popular, I automatically assumed that the bitch that brought the cup of ice without him even asking was on some shady shit.

"I'm good. I'm going to get some ice from the inside."

I walked away; I don't know if they thought I was stuck up or what, but I could feel all eyes on me as I switched my ass to the restaurant. I went straight to the bar, got myself a cup of ice, and came back out. The music was playing, laughter in the air, people just shooting the breeze. The vibe was all good. Between the Grey goose and atmosphere, I was having a good ass time. Glad I came.

"I'm about to order something to eat now."

Jeremiah reached in his pocket and pulled out a small wad, not what I'm used to, but I'll take it. He handed me $40. I rolled my eyes. $40.00 bucks, wow. Small-time.

"What kind of wings do you want?"

"Baby, I don't eat meat. Just get me some fries and get some celery and carrots on the side."

"All right."

I placed my order inside, mingled with a few from school, and then found my way outside. I didn't see Jeremiah.

"This nigga." I griped when the black monster truck pulled up into the parking lot. Kissing my teeth, I pretended like I hadn't noticed him. It was Julius. We haven't spoken since he dissed me last week—old nerd ass.

He parked right across from us. Through the dark tent, I wondered if he saw me. I looked straight ahead as if I didn't see him.

"You mean to tell me my nigga let your fine ass get up out of his eyesight?"

I chuckled at the skinny dude in front of me. He had a blue and gold jacket representing the same bike club Jeremiah was from.

"I'm a big girl," I replied, batting my eyes. In no form or fashion was he my type. High yellow dudes with big lips didn't do it for me, but his company beat standing there looking stupid.

"You more than a big girl, you are all woman, damn you fine." He flirted. "He always gets the good ones."

"Nah, baby, he ain't got me. We are simply friends." I countered with a slight attitude.

He licked his lips, "well, let me get your number."

"Nope," I replied, walking off. I was going to check on my wings and chill with those I knew from school. I'd catch up with Jeremiah whenever.

Stepping back into the restaurant, my stomach growled at the smell of chicken. I couldn't wait to bite into my lemon pepper wings. Bobbing my head to Plies, I made my way over to the pickup counter. Happy that my order was ready, I got my food and scanned the dining area for a spot to eat. Up against the wall at the high table, I placed my wings down. With quickness, I opened them and began to devour my food. A girl named Crystal from my political science class walked up. Whispering in my ear, she asked for a wing. I nodded my head yeah. Occasionally, I darted my head toward the door, wondering if Jeremiah's ass was coming in.

"You want a drink?" Crystal asked.

"A beer," I replied. She nodded and disappeared.

I looked around to see who I could ask to take me home. It damn sure wasn't Julius.

"Hmph," I mumbled, eyes on the dance floor. It was him. He was the only white boy in the place. No glasses on, red baseball cap, a tight long sleeve graphic shirt, skinny jeans, and vans. His dance partner was a light-skinned chick who looked to be mixed by her long crinkly hair. She was freaking all over him like she wasn't wearing a short-ass skirt that kept rising up. JuJu had his hands around her waist, guiding her. He wasn't smiling, but he was all into it, most definitely enjoying himself.

'Nerdy, weird-ass white boy, I care nothing about,' I thought to myself. I will admit I felt a hint of jealousy.

"Here, girl," Crystal handed me a beer. Briefly looking at it before taking it, my eyes landed back on JuJu. Ol' girl was touching her toes, bouncing all up on his crotch . I could've run circles around that hoe, but I wasn't in competition.

"Word around campus, he got a big dick." Crystal spoke into my ear.

I almost choked on my beer.

"Girl, stop." I waved Crystal off with a laugh. She shrugged.

The song changed, and they stopped dancing. I rolled my eyes when she put her arms around Ju's neck. 'I guess,' I thought as I turned and went back outside.

Jeremiah was talking to his boys drinking from a white cup. I stormed up to him.

"That was rude, ask me out, and you just disappear." He looked at me and chuckled before looking back at his boys.

"These hoes ain't got no manners." He implied.

I stepped back. Placed my hands on my hips.

"Excuse me." I snapped.

"Aye, bro, she must've missed the memo; you don't love these hoes." One of his friends said.

I got ready to respond, but Jeremiah's outburst stopped me.

"Nigga don't be disrespecting my bitch." He glared at his boy.

I don't know if it was something in the air or if these niggas were just weirdos.

"Who are you talking about? I'm not your bitch. Nigga fuck you." I stormed off.

I was yanked by my arm. Turning around, I swung on the nigga with my free hand.

"You better stop hitting me, or I'm going to hit you back." He warned.

"Nigga, do it." The deep voice warned. " , Let her arm go."

I didn't have time to digest how Ju looked like he was with all the shits. Because when the word nigga left his mouth, about five of Jeremiah's biker friends were surrounding him.

I was nervous as fuck. I was mad at a JuJu for how he left me hanging that night, but he was my buddy. He always helped me with my studies when I needed it. We would kick it in between classes while I ran my mouth about my weekend or trips back to Cali. Besides not picking me up that night, he was cool. I didn't want him to get beat up.

"What you just say, white boy? Say that shit again." Jeremiah bellowed.

"Toya, go get in my truck," Ju ordered, eyes still on Jeremiah.

He held so much authority in his tone. I was ready to obey his orders, but I wasn't about to leave him. He was in this mess because of me. I had to have his back.

"She ain't getting in shit, white boy." Jeremiah grabbed my arm again. Next thing you know, all hell broke loose. JuJu swung, and Jeremiah stumbled back. One of Jeremiah's boys ran up, and JuJu was fighting both of them. He was straight hanging. The white boy had hands. When the lanky nigga blindsided him, he stumbled slightly but still handled his. I ran up and started swinging on Jeremiah. But I was knocked down when a bunch of guys ran up and started jumping Ju.

Thank God, police sirens could be heard in the distance. Them punks scattered. They jumped on their bikes and left.

All of them were on him and couldn't even knock him down. Although he did have a busted lip, his hat came off, and I even saw a scratch on his red face.

"Oh my God, JUJU, are you ok?" I asked.

"Didn't I tell you to get in the truck?" he roared.

I nodded yes.

"Where're your keys? Let me drive you." I offered.

I'm good. He wiped his mouth with the hem of his shirt.

"Toya, go get in the car." He yelled.

By then, the cops pulled up. I felt so bad as I watched from his truck while he talked to the police . Within five minutes, we were pulling off.

" I'm sorry."

He didn't say anything. Instead, he stared ahead, with a cold expression.

"I'm going to have my brothers handle them for us."

"I don't need another man handling shit. Who the fuck do you think I am? Some lame-ass white boy. I got brothers. I don't need them either."

"I didn't say that," I muttered .

"You was talking all that shit on the phone. I should've…"

"You should've what?"

"Toya, be quiet before you say some stupid shit that pisses me off."

I parted my lips to say something…

"Toya, I'm not in the mood for your shit." He warned.

I rolled my eyes and crossed my arms over my chest. Huffing and puffing because I wanted to say something so bad.

We drove in silence. I didn't speak up until I noticed we had passed our school.

"Where are we going?" I asked.

"Does it matter?" he replied.

"What's your problem? Just because you boss'd up on them niggas don't mean you get to talk to me crazy."

"Toya didn't I ask you to hush?" he looked at me, jaws tight, glaring hard.

"Take me home," I ordered.

"Fo sho." He turned the music up and busted a U turn. I couldn't stop staring at him. He was tripping. I have not ever seen him act like this. I didn't even know he had it in him. So, low key, I was turned on.

There was something about a man who displayed authority.

When we made it to campus, he pulled in front of my lot. Without saying a word, I could tell he just wanted me out.

"Get out." He barked.

"No," I replied.

"Toya gone. I had enough of you tonight. You wanted me to bring you home; you're here."

His voice was laced with annoyance. He took a deep breath and exhaled . When he closed his eyes and laid his head back on his seat, I knew he was fed up with me. I know I can be a handful , but it's not my fault. I'm the only girl, and I am spoiled. I just like having things my way. I also knew when I was wrong, and depending on the situation, I would admit it. JuJu has been nothing but a good person to me. Unfortunately, he got his ass jumped trying to help me.

"Look, I'm sorry, sorry for talking crazy. I know you were just trying to help me. We are friends. I don't mind going where you were taking me. I trust you."

"Cool. But I no longer want your company." He replied, eyes focused ahead.

My heart sank in my stomach. Julius really just hurt my feelings.

"Wow!" I muttered.

He roared his engine.

"I don't care about you doing that. I ain't getting out."

Ring... ring... my eyes darted toward the digital display on the dash. My nose flared, reading, "incoming call Florida Pussy."

He answered the call from his steering wheel.

"What up." Eyes still closed. He was acting like he was the shit.

"Boo, I heard what happened. Are you good?" A female voice answered.

"Yeah. I'm straight." He replied.

"Are you hurt?" She inquired. She sounded too concerned for me.

"I'm good." He assured her.

"I can't believe they jumped you. Where are you?"

The hoe was getting on my nerves.

"Dropping my friend off." If looks could kill, he would've been dead.

"Oh, ok. Can you come over?"

"Yeah. I might. I need to shower and shit."

"I have the stuff I got you for Christmas you never took. So, you can shower here and change." Bitch sounded desperate.

"Let me go," I said, opening the door. I had enough.

When I jumped down, I thought he would say something. Instead, I heard the girl,

"See you soon, boo." She cooed.

"Bet." He replied.

I didn't bother to shut the door; I stormed off. I entered my apartment; the light coming from my candles was just enough for me to maneuver around. I was lightweight tipsy, but Ju pissed me off so bad I needed another drink. I stomped to the kitchen cussing the entire way. After I made myself a glass of Hennessy, I went back into the living room. My cellphone was ringing. It better not have been Jeremiah or JuJu. I didn't have shit to say to either one of them. It was Bishop. My boo from L.A.

"Hello." I gulped my drink.

"What's up, baby? What are you doing?"

"Nothing just got home."

"Good. I'm out here. Come see me."

"You out here?"

"Yeah, got some business to handle with my boy. I'm leaving back out tomorrow night."

"Send me your location; I'll be there."

***

"Who in the hell got you cheesing?" I snapped, standing in front of the door, looking Bishop up and down. Annoyed as all outdoors, I still couldn't deny how handsome he was. Bishop was tall, dark, and sexy. I was never fond of dudes with dreads, but the long blonde locks look so damn good on him. He is a little on the chunky side but wore that shit well. Stayed dressing to the nines, always smelled good, pockets fat, and a thick dick he knows how to use well.

The two of us have been dealing with the other for almost a year. I met him at the mall, I was with Candy. All it took was for him to tell the cashier in the

LV store he got me for me to notice him. Nigga's loved to floss and I'm the bitch that didn't mind as long as it was beneficial to me.

Bishop slid his phone back into his pocket. With a smirk on his face, he walked up on me.

"Cute ass." He said kissing me on the lips. "Come in." He stepped to the side.

"Not until you tell me who got you smiling?" I faked mad.

"I'm laughing off the homeboy. You wanna see?"

"No, just tell me." I folded my arms across my chest.

"My homeboy Ghost. The ones I'm out here to link with. Nigga got me laughing complaining about how women are crazy, and he will never get married."

"And that's funny?" I pushed passed him walking into the room.

"Yeah. For him to be complaining about a chick he gotta be feeling her. Ghost don't care about nothing but his money."

"Oh," I said flopping down on the couch." The 2-bedroom suite he had was nice. Always top of the line.

"What's wrong   little momma?" he asked stepping behind me to rub my shoulders. I started to tell him what went down with Jeremiah and Julius, but I changed my mind. Although I wanted a male's opinion about the way Julius acted. One minute he wanted to protect me and ride with him and the next he was putting me out of his car. Was I really the issue? But I decided not to even go there with Bishop; I mean he's not my man but we rock how we rock and I don't wanna disrespect him.

" I'm annoyed because my roommate talking about she's moving out and I have to come up with the rest of the money. " The lie rolled off my tongue with ease. Now my roommate was hardly ever home because of her girlfriend but she wasn't moving out and she paid rent faithfully.

"Man, I know you not wasting the little time we got tonight on nonsense when I'm right here. All you gotta do is tell me what you need. I know I'm not your man and you ain't my girl, but I gotcha little mama, you should already know that."

Bishop came from behind the couch and stood in front of me. Gently took me by the hand ushering me to stand. Chills washed over my body just looking at him and to know what he was about to do to me made me forget all the issues I had with the two lames.

"I know boo, thank you." He pressed his mouth against mine, and we began to kiss. I was enjoying every moment. We rubbed all over each other, moaning both enjoying what was taking place. Bishop and I have never shared anything that felt remotely passionate. Without notice, I broke our kiss. As I stared into his eyes, I was trying to find the answers to my questions; is he upset about how I stopped what we were sharing? Is he feeling me? He offered a warm smile.

"What you got to drink?" I asked breaking the awkward silence.

"You already know," he said walking over to the bar grabbing a bottle of Casamigos.

"Pour up, so I can go take a shower."

After he made my drink, he sat down to roll himself a blunt. I thanked him and headed to the shower.

"Order room service or something, I'm hungry." I tossed over my shoulder.

"Anything for you baby." He replied

I smiled, Bishop knows he loves him some Toya and as long as he stays spoiling me, he can have me whenever he likes.

Julius

"Fuck." I roared, smashing away from Toya's spot. That chick is a fucking headache; got me out here fighting to defend her ass and shit. I respect women, but I don't fight over or for no females. I knew her ass was trouble when I laid eyes on her. Her sexy ass was a dancer at a club I was checking out for business reasons. Off back, I recognized her ass, the cute chick from my history class who's always late. Being co-owner of two strip clubs in Cali for the last five years, I am not new to this. I have been around bad females all my life. I ain't the type of dude to slide up in pussy just because I can, and I'm picky with my dick. I ain't trying to catch shit, plus once you bless these women with that good dick, they lose all the little sense they have left. I ain't trying to claim nobody right now.

Don't give a fuck what none of y'all think. Ain't gotta explain who I am because you already heard about me---Geeky. Rich. White boy with more confidence than these loudmouth, flashy, designer-wearing hoe niggas y'all be falling in love with.

Back to Toya, she bad. Body. Looks. And the way she worked that pole had me ignoring her ghetto ways and imagining her being my freaky hood girl. What worked in my favor is that I knew for a fact I ain't her type. She is a gold digger and, just like most chicks from the hood, in love with thugs. It wasn't that I am not confident, far from the truth, but Toya would be my weakness. She would have me doing shit out of

101

the norm, like choking her ass out for not listening. The girl already got me ready to body niggas. Something about them pretty ass, sexy ass hood girls that drive a man crazy. Toya is all that and then some. Fuck around and have me breaking all the rules for her.

"Something told me to let her ass fail. Shouldn't have even helped her ungrateful ass." I scolded myself. As I maneuvered in and out of traffic, I thought about when Toya first approached me.

The next day after seeing her at the club, she asked if I could tutor her. I have a good heart, I help when I can, but for Toya, I knew it was best that I stay away from her. I told her straight up no, but of course, her crazy ass wouldn't take no for an answer. My good heart, an unrevealed weakness for her, and persistence won me over. Tutoring led to us grabbing something to eat, chilling on the grass between classes, and sitting next to each other in class. Eventually, we exchanged numbers, and the next thing you know, I was picking her up whenever she was stranded or too drunk to drive home from the club. She even called me when she had men issues. She would get mad if they didn't give her money or wanted to fuck her for free. She vented to me about all that. Toya was toxic and poison combined- if that's possible. I can sense the outcome, and I'm not even trying to go there with her. Glad I put her out. Gotta stay away from that girl.

I pulled up to my snow bunny's crib and parked in the driveway—nothing like getting some good ass head to relieve stress.

"Man, chill with that," I said, shaking my head at how I wished Toya was the one that was about to top me off. Visualizing her pretty face staring up at me while deep throating me had me ready to bust- you know you have to be bad if you can make a nigga ready to bust just by thinking of you.

Glancing at the time on my dash, I figured Bishop should've made it in town and checked into his hotel by now. Pulling my work phone from the center console, I put in my password and saw a text confirming that he had arrived two hours ago.

Me: You good?

Bishop: Yeah, rested. About to have my little bitch come over.

Me: Man, these females will drive you crazy if you let them. I swear, I ain't ever getting married. Hoes out here weird.

Bishop: LOL what bitch got you in your feelings?

Me: No one. I will get w/u tomorrow.

Bishop: Be safe.

I thought about having Bishop ride up on them niggas with me, but nah; I'll handle them on my own. Bishop and I had to send the bitch who claimed rape a message. That's why he was out here.

Tossing the phone back in the console, my chick for the night's porch light came on.

Stormy

The hot water cascaded over my body. I inhaled and exhaled several times enjoying the aroma of the peppermint shower bomb, trying to release the built-up tension. Typically, when I began to feel this overwhelmed, either a holiday, my mother's birthday, or the anniversary of her death was coming up. However, it was April, so that wasn't the case. The heaviness I was feeling was something I had control over but have yet to correct the issue. Rotating my neck in a circular motion, I thought about my life and if I am doing enough to get where I desired to be. I had days when I felt like my life was good. My bank account wasn't lacking. I had a decent gig at the firm, and I taught dance. I had the ideal mate- a corporate man who knew the value of hard work and cared about his family. Blake would never put me in the type of situation my father put my mother in. And he was nothing like Deon. Then some days, I felt like I was stuck. I could see my ending and headed in that direction, but it was taking too long to get my happily ever after. After three years, Blake and I still aren't living together nor planning a wedding. I was tired of hiding the truth, but Blake insisted that it was the best way for now. I understood we were to wait for him to make partner, but damn. I think his dad was holding us back on purpose. He didn't want his son with a black chick, but what could he do--- nothing. His old ass was also holding me up from opening my studio.

Blake wanted me to wait until after he made partner for that too. Our career launch he wanted to do together. I was following my man's lead, so, I had to be patient- but for how long?

A cool breeze entered the shower causing my nipples to harden; Blake made his way inside, wrapping his arms around my waist from behind—a sensual kiss was placed on the back of my neck. I could feel his hard-on poking me in my behind.

"Mmm." His hands massaged my center, and I moaned, anticipating an orgasm. I could almost feel it. He just about had it figured out but not quite. Taking his hand, I guided Blake to my pearl.

"Right there, baby. Add pressure and rub it slow," I whispered, rotating my hips desperately wanting to cum.

My eyes were closed, one hand over my head rubbing Blake's hair. "A little faster." I moaned. I like to get mine first because if my baby gets too excited and busts before me, I will have to wait until he was hard again.

"Nah, baby. Take this good cock." Blake ordered, pulling away from me. "Bend over," he said, stepping back—one hand on my ass cheek, the other he used to guide his penis inside my wetness. Instantly I tightened my walls. He loved when I did that.

"Ahhh shit." He moaned.

My left hand was planted on the wall, and with the other I pleasured myself. I was a pro at pleasing myself. My man pumped in and out of my gushy center. " Ohhhh shit, I'm cumming…" I cried.

Blake groaned as he pumped in and out of me. Within minutes I was having a full-blown orgasm, and Blake was spitting his seeds all over my ass. I could go for another round, but I knew he didn't have time.

———

Falling by Alicia Keys played as Blake and I traveled in his Tesla. We were headed to his parent's house. His mom wanted me to join her for a ladies' brunch. I didn't want to go, and Blake knew it. I didn't like her best friend, whom I was sure would be there, and I hated to be around his father for obvious reasons. But I agreed, because Blake was tagging along. He claimed to have wanted to spend time with his father. I didn't make it to the party, so I sucked it up. Gotta be a good girlfriend to the man you love.

"Baby, have you ever thought about going back to school?" Blake asked out of the blue. I could feel him looking at me.

"Not really. No." I said, looking over at him. His eyes were back on the road.

"You should." He stated.

"Why? I have a degree." I lightweight snapped.

"I know. I was there when you graduated. Have you thought about getting a degree you could use?"

"What?" I yelled, totally shocked he would belittle my choice of study.

I don't know what the hell he was shaking his head for. He's the one who was talking stupid — insulting me like it was cool. Now, all of a sudden, my degree wasn't shit. His fucking career was going to his head.

"I'm just saying. I mean. There are plenty of people with multiple degrees." He tried to play down the bullshit he was saying.

"Well, it ain't me, I don't need another degree. My shit will work just fine for me. I would've been had my studio open if I wasn't waiting on you." I snapped; my face frowned up.

We stopped at a red light. Blake looked at me with a surprised expression.

"So, you're blaming me because you aren't successful?" He ridiculed.

"Excuse me?" I retorted; this man was trying me today.

"Nothing. Leave it alone." He pulled off, driving fast like he had a right to be mad.

I glared at him. I wanted to go off. Ask him who's been in his ear talking shit about me. Blake has never come at me like that. When we first got together, he supported my dream to become a famous dance teacher, now the bitch was acting brand new.

"Yeah. I'm going to leave it alone." I looked out the window rolling my eyes. Only if he knew I was fighting the inner demons that wanted to come out and give this asshole a reality check. Tell him about his pussy ass flaws. Thank God for therapy. After losing my mother, I was angry. When I was in college, I got help with controlling my anger. Otherwise, I probably would have popped his ass in the head. He was the damn fraud.

Everyone knew Blake didn't want to be a got-damn lawyer. He dreamed of going to the NBA. He was a damn good player. However, his father practically forced him to become a lawyer, and his ass did—stupid ass.

" I love you, Stormy. I just-"

Right on cue, my phone rung. I answered it. I didn't want to hear shit else he had to say.

"Hey, sis?" Toya greeted.

"What's wrong?" I asked, picking up on her dry tone.

"No, what's wrong with you?"

"Nothing. In the car with Blake." I spat dryly.

"Why did you say it like that?" Blake snapped. He could be a crybaby at times. I ignored his ass.

"Girl, what's the problem?" Toya asked.

"No problem at all, sis."

"Oh, that's Toya. I should've known." He said snidely.

"Anyways. I have my own white boy issues." She confessed.

"What?" I laughed. I heard her I was just shocked she admitted it.

"Girl, I texted him to talk first and then another to apologize, and he left me at seen both times."

"Let me find out." I teased.

"Find out nothing. He's a friend. Call me when you're alone. Love you." She said before hanging up.

I chuckled a little longer than expected. There was no way Toya was in her feelings about, as she called him, a nerd. A white one at that.

While Blake was venting about me taking things out of context, I was daydreaming about who this guy was. Toya wanted to act like she didn't like him. The way she talks about JuJu, complaining about their little argument and how he's ignoring her, I say my sister is feeling him. Good for her. She needed to stay away from the thugs she loved.

As we approached Blake's parent's mansion, the black iron gate with a cursive "W" slowly opened. I mentally prepared myself for the day.

"Stormy, I apologize. I love you, and I'm sorry if I offended you." Blake confessed.

My mind drifted back to everything he said. Suppose that's how he really felt, cool. However, I wouldn't put up with him disrespecting me. He felt how he felt about my career, and I thought he had given up on his dream to please his father.

"I love you too," I replied... "I forgive you." Blake stopped the car, leaned over, and kissed me. Slipping his tongue inside my mouth.

———————

"Welcome." Mrs. Whitman greeted us; we were standing at the front door. She smiled and ushered for us to come inside.

She was donned in Versace leggings with the matching jacket and 6-inch-high heels. Her hair was pulled back into a slick ponytail. I would always refer to her as a Diva. I wasn't quite sure of her age. She didn't have a cake on the two birthdays I spent with her, and her age was never a topic. If I had to guess, I would say she was in her late 50's. I liked that she wasn't one of those stiff rich white women who wore formal attire every day.

"Thank you for having us, and I love that perfume," I complimented , walking into her awaiting arms, and we hugged.

"Hi, mommy." Blake greeted, hugging her as well and placing a kiss on her cheek.

Once entirely inside the house, I glanced to my right. I saw Mr. Whitman standing at the top of the stairs. Apart from the salt and pepper hair and age difference, he and Blake looked just alike. He was donned in a white polo shirt tucked into a pair of tan dockers. He stood with a cigar in his mouth, eyes on his son.

"Jr., after you speak to the guest, come and see me," his deep voice boomed. Then, he turned around and walked off.

"Hello, father. I'll be right there." Blake called behind him.

The man hardly ever spoke to me. It bothered me because I would be the mother of his grandchildren one day. Blake needed to nip it in the bud now.

"Come, we are out back."

We trailed behind Mrs. Whitman into the backyard. The yard was beautiful, but the setup was even nicer. (describe what you see)

"Hey, Blake." The two women gushed , smiling and waving. I recognized Michelle. She's Mrs. Whitman's best friend. A black lady who resembles the actor, Vanessa Williams. The Asian chick wasn't familiar at all. She looked to be around my age. Pretty I would say.

"Hello, ladies," Blake replied, walking over to where they were sitting. Both women stood. One by one, they hugged him.

"Stormy, that's Jamie. Michelle's niece."

"Hey." She spoke and sat back down.

I didn't bother to return the half-ass greeting.

Mrs. Whitman talked about a girl's brunch, and it's only us four. So, the only thing I was going to enjoy was the variety of food and mimosas.

Blake excused himself. I glanced over at the Jamie girl, and she was looking at my man's ass. Something told me this was going to be an interesting day.

"That's all me." I tossed.

"Excuse me?" Jamie replied.

"You were staring at my man's ass. That's all me." I replied bluntly.

She chuckled.

"I'm engaged. I am not interested in Blake."

"Stormy, you've been Blake's girlfriend for a few years now. So, Jamie shouldn't be a threat." Michelle tossed.

I gawked at Michelle, catching the shade and returning it.

"Says the woman who can't keep a man."

"Oh my. Ladies. Stop." Mrs. Whitman jumped in. Her hand was over her chest.

Silence took over. I picked up my flute and began to sip.

"Stormy, what do you do?" The chick asked.

"I teach dance."

"That's cool. Do you own your studio?"

"No, she's still working on that," Michelle said.

That jab hurt.

"Michelle. That's enough. I won't allow you to disrespect my future daughter-in-law. I mean it."

"How far in the future are you talking about?" She continued with the shade.

"That's your last warning." Mrs. Whitman squinted her eyes.

"Ok, ok, I'll behave," Michelle promised.

Michelle's words had me stuck. Everything she was saying was what I'd been feeling. I guess that's why it hurt so bad.

"I'm going to give you that one. But that's your last time disrespecting me." I sneered; standing from my seat. I made my way to the buffet. Totally in my feelings. As they say, the truth hurts.

I felt someone approaching. From the corner of my eye, I could see it was Michelle. I hoped she knew that I would whoop her ass. I learned how to shoot and box when I was nine. I was good at both. So, she better not try me.

"You're black, and I'm black," I looked at her and rolled my eyes.

Yeah, bitch I know that.

"I'm hard on you because you make me mad." She spoke in a hushed tone.

I looked at her as if she was crazy; how in the hell did I make her mad?

"I see myself in you. You depend on Blake to complete you. Like being with him will give you the perfect life. Being with a man that supports you, values you, and loves you for you is the perfect love story, Stormy. You are waiting on him to marry you. He hasn't even proposed. Why haven't you opened your studio? Is it because he won't give you the money or do you have it, and he suggests you wait? I bet he's trying to change you. Stay woke. Pay attention... Eventually, you'll forget who you are and end up like me." She chuckled. "You'll look in the mirror and wonder how you've become one of them. When I look at you, I see who I used to be. Strong. Confident. And looking for that perfect love story. Girlfriend, don't settle." She walked off.

Michelle's speech stuck in my head. I tried to ignore her assumptions, but she hit everything on the mark. By the time I was on my third glass of champagne , I no longer gave a damn. I wasn't losing myself. I was being patient. And I was going to set

113

deadlines for Blake to step up. Shockingly the rest of our time went well. Michelle barely spoke, which was good. Mrs. Whitman was in and out of the conversation; whoever she was texting had most of her attention.

Jamie and I conversed. I learned she was from the UK. She and her fiancé separated for two years. She didn't say why. She turned out to be cool. I don't know if it was the champagne, or if I just enjoyed her company that much. I accepted an invite to a sponsored trip to Fiji with Blake's approval.

When I came to my senses, I suggested to Blake that he cancel our invite, but he refused. His excuse was we haven't been on vacation in forever, and it'll be rude to cancel.

So here I was, three days later, on her private jet with a bunch of stuck-up couples. Michelle and Mrs. Whitman came along too. Though, no sun, I put my shades on and mentally prepared myself for the flight.

"Blake, that's a nice color on you. It complements your eyes." Jamie said.

My head popped up. I looked at Blake, who was sitting next to me, smiling.

"Thanks, Jamie. I thought the same thing when I picked it out." I butted in.

"Right." She countered.

"Jamie, is he coming this time?" Michelle asked.

"Of course, auntie. He's running late. He will be here. After all, it's his idea. My fiancé will be here." She grinned, I caught her cutting her eyes at me.

"I won't hold my breath," Michelle mumbled.

Michelle's ass was something else. I laid my head back and tried to go to sleep while everyone else began to make conversation amongst themselves.

"There's the man responsible for such an amazing trip." Jamie gushed.

"I'm going to the back," the deep voice announced, annoyance on full display.

MY HEART DROPPED when I lifted my head to look at her man. I was not expecting to see Ross's rude-ass client "Lloyd Dyce. As if he could feel me looking at him, he looked my way. His hard stare softened. Taking his bottom lip into his mouth, slowly his eyes roamed from my Burberry sneakers to my bare thighs, pausing at my breasts.

This man was fucking me with his eyes in front of all these people, including his woman and my man.

"Take off your glasses." He ordered, voice deep, eyes hard.

I could feel Blake's eyes on me. Everyone in the front of the jet was staring, I was sure trying to figure out what was up between the two of us. Jamie had a confused look on her face. I didn't blame her; I was just as confused.

"Dyce, is there a reason you need my woman to take off her glasses?" Blake asked.

He knew him. Well, he was Ross's client.

"Remove your shades." He repeated, completely ignoring everyone. It was the way he said it like if I didn't, I would be punished. I removed my shades. He gave me a hard stare, followed by a reverse nod, and walked off. What in the world.

"Do you know him? Was he a part of your father's drug game?"

Blake's comment not only shocked me but embarrassed me as well. I'm sure everyone heard him.

"I don't know him asshole." I jumped up and walked to the opposite side of the jet from him. Something was telling me to get off and go home. Instead, I took my ass to Fiji, and I think it was because Lloyd was going.

Lloyd

"You sure about this shit?" I asked Boss. My gut was telling me this shit wasn't a good idea. But, before I expressed my thoughts, I wanted to give Boss a chance to make sense.

"Yeah, I'm sure. He fucked up and paid the price. We found out it wasn't him who snaked us but his boy." He said, looking at me from the passenger seat of my truck. We were in the back of a warehouse Boss recently purchased. "So, it's his fault but not his fault." He shrugged. "Pops even said he brought us in a lot of money. With Geo and them locked up, we need a nigga like him to replace them."

"He's a fucking crack head," I spoke through tight teeth; I was trying my best not to go off. But he was in charge. I was out of the game, only stepping in when stupid shit like this was going on.

"That man has been clean. I verified that," he chuckled.
"It wasn't crack. He was a drunk. Do you blame him? His wife was killed in his face." Boss reminded me. Until this day, I hated he did that shit, but I never spoke on it.

10 years ago

"Are you ready?" I asked, looking at him.

"Yup." He replied, pulling his black ski mask over his face.

"Don't do no cupcake shit. Make him regret ever playing with us. Being in the game ain't just about money, fast cars, and hoes." I lectured.

"I know, man, kill or be killed. Calculate every step. Death or prison can be my ending. No one gets a pass when it comes to money, not even family. Don't trust no one, not even you." He repeated what I'd been telling him for years. It was the same shit our parents engraved in me.

"Glad you've been listening."

"Look, man. Let's just do this shit. I got a bad little bitch waiting on me to slide through."

I chuckled.

"You love them, strippers. I hope you're strapping up."

"Maaannn... A bitch can't even suck my dick if I ain't got no condom. And the hoe jaws weak, I'm kicking her to the curb."

I grinned as I shook my head. Bro was wild. He was way worse than me when I was sixteen. I wasn't paranoid or nothing, but I like to be on point—no room for slip-ups. So, we went over the plan one last time.

We climbed out of the car in army fatigue pants, long black sleeve T-shirst, and wheat Timbs. We lightly jogged across the street, ducked low, and made our way across the yard to the back gate. I was the first to jump the fence, and he followed. When we reached the back door, and little bro popped the locks with a fucking credit card, all I could do was shake my head. Goat has been in the game since I was in diapers. In his hood, he was the man. In my opinion, his paper wasn't as long as it should've been, but he had money. The nigga was an idiot. For one, he still lived in the hood, meaning everybody knew where he laid his head. Two, he didn't even have a sound surveillance system; there was no way we should've been able to get up on him this easy. Lastly, he was too got-damn old, seen too much not to know greed would be the demise of any man. If the old ass nigga had the audacity to steal from my family, he must've thought he was untouchable. No one was untouchable, not even me. Effortlessly we moved through the kitchen. Our eyes connected as we tip-toed up the stairs. When hit the corner, a bedroom door was open and a dim light was on. We both shrugged as we aimed our guns and marched into the room.

"Oh my god." His wife screamed when she saw us. She was sitting at a desk with her phone in hand.

"Put it down," I ordered, snatching the phone from her and powering it off. She was frantic. Her hands were in the air, eyes closed, as she prayed.

My partner in crime, Boss, stood over Goat. The nigga was snoring like he didn't have a care in the world. Then, just when I was wondering how long the nigga would stand there, he began to hit Goat over the head with his gun.

"What the fuck." He groaned. Eyes wide with fear, he jumped up in the bed. "Just don't hurt my wife." He said, looking over at her.

"Nigga you don't get to negotiate." Boss roared.

Wham

Wham

My brother hit him over the head several times. Blood gushed down his face.

"Please, please, please, what is going on? Why are they fucking with us?" The wife cried.

"Nigga I need my 500 racks or you, this bitch, and whoever else is in this motha fucka is dead." My brother bellowed; voice laced with venom.

I stared at him, having never seen him like this before. I felt a little bit bad because I felt like I made him like this. He's been watching me all his life and now look

"You come in my house and disrespect me and think I'm going to pay." Goat had the audacity to say.

My brother yanked him out of bed. His body fell to the floor, making a loud thumping sound.

"Nigga you think you hard," Boss yelled, kicking him a few times. I could hear him grunt and moan.

"Just tell them where the money is." The wife cried. "Our daughter will be home soon- Fuck pride, my child is more important." She began to sob.

Lifting him from the floor , he was ordered again to pay up.

"I don't got it. I swear."

"Wrong answer. Since I gotta live without my bread, you'll live every day regretting this."

Before I could register the warning, little mutha fucka aimed and fired a bullet to the ol' girl's head. Shot her while I was standing that close.

"Nooooo!" Goat yelled.

"What the fuck." I jumped back. Looking at the nigga like he was crazy as he began to pistol whip Goat again.

"Let's go." I roared.

I wasn't feeling the wife being killed, but I respected Boss's call. His job was to collect or make the nigga regret he ever crossed us.

"Look, it's a stupid idea. You are playing with a lot of people's lives, bringing him in. You don't know what he on." I blared.

"You paranoid. The nigga wanna eat. He ain't on nothing else." Boss assumed.

Pinching the bridge of my nose, I tried my best to calm down.

"Did you talk to your little brother about this?" It wasn't my decision. I handed the keys to Boss.

"Nah." He replied.

"Do it," I demanded.

"Ju rolls with me, but I'll do it." He said with confidence.

A black SUV turned into the alley.

"You invited him here?" I looked at him.

"Yeah."

"Get out," I ordered. I didn't want to be anywhere around that nigga. "If you do it, don't ever bring me up. I'm done with the empire completely. No more advice, no nothing."

"Whatever, man." Boss climbed out of the truck, "have a safe trip. But I won't forget how you left me hanging."

I revved my engine, letting him know I was done with the conversation.

"Run this by J, do not go behind his back on this. Tell him everything." I glared at him, waiting for a response.

"I am. Damn!" He replied, walking off.

Boss had me heated. If he went through with the shit, it'd affect us all. I may not be in the game anymore, but I've done enough to get myself hung. My gut was telling me this shit was going to backfire. There is no way he should be comfortable doing business with that dude again. Granted, it was years ago, a mutha fucka could never forget that night tho.

I was heavily geared toward calling Jamie and telling her to go without me. I didn't feel like being around anybody but my thoughts. Maneuvering in and out of traffic, I thought about it a few more times. Fiji would be perfect for getting away. The water always calmed me. I was almost an hour late, but I didn't give a fuck. My pilot wasn't going to make any moves without me.

I pulled up to the private airport, hopped out, grabbed my bags, and made my way up the steps onto the jet. I frowned upon seeing the unexpected faces. Who in the fuck told her to invite all these people? I told her-her aunt and a friend only. I hope she didn't think we would be doing no couple shit.

"Finally," Michelle mumbled. I gave her a look that she ignored.

Jamie announced me being responsible for the trip. It was that perfume again. I smelled her before I saw her.

When my eyes landed on her, a nigga heart swelled. Behind the glasses, I knew it was her. I studied her face a million times since the first and last time I saw her. That fucking mole on her lip. Them thick ass thighs. My dick was hard as fuck. So, when she obeyed by taking her glasses off, she turned me on. She was getting fucked on this trip, and it wouldn't be by punk ass Blake Whitman.

I heard the smart-ass comment he made to Stormy. My first thought was to put his punk ass off my jet. I'd get more satisfaction knowing he was on the same island while I fucked his woman. I guess I made a good call on this trip after all.

Toya

I was leaving my last class headed to the library to get some studying done before I began my weekend escapade. I was dressed in boyfriend jeans, a white half top, covered by a flannel I took off after class and wrapped around my waist. On my feet are a pair of Nike sandals. A blue hat to the back representing my university covering my curly main. It rained the night before, but now the sun was out, displaying a beautiful sunny day.

Strolling across campus, vaguely peeping at what was going on around me, I was deeply thinking. I had to come up with this money quickly. My father needed me. There was an ample opportunity on the table. As always, I had his back. I was going to the new strip club they opened in Saint Pete to make the rest of the money.

Allow me to introduce myself----- officially. Just in case you forgot, I am Toya, Stormy's stepsister. Because of how close we are, you would think we have been around each other all our lives. My brothers and I didn't meet her until I was fifteen and her eighteen. I'm my parent's only daughter. I have a twin brother, and our older brother is 32; 5 years our senior. I'm close with both of my brothers. My mother and I are cool. When time permits, we spend time together. When we do hang out, it's nothing but laughs and fun. Now, I'm a daddy's girl. I love my father with all my heart—he's my hero. In my eyes, he can do no wrong. His flaws and a few mishaps may have left a bad taste in Stormy's mouth, but he's human and my father. I respect my sister for not dealing with daddy. It's her choice.

I'm a 24-year-old college student. Fine and sexy. I didn't have to pay for my perfect body because I got it from my momma. I'm single, but I have plenty of guy friends. I fuck with get money niggas who will give to me when my hand is out. My mommy and daddy taught me that. Call me a gold digger but I ain't fuckin' with no broke nigga. You already know I'm a stripper. I started when I was in high school. I didn't have to; my brothers stepped up when daddy fell off. And they are still doing it while I'm in college. If they found out I had been dancing JUST to help daddy, shit would hit the fan. They would probably cut me off or trip on my father. It wasn't happening. I'm glad they live in Baltimore. They will be down for Mother's Day, and I am going to for sure have them pay a visit to my old club. The bitches ain't getting away with taking from me. Oh, and my major is psychology.

About 30 feet ahead, I spotted this white boy in a pair of red Bermuda shorts, a fitted black graphic T, and a red baseball cap to the back. He was talking to two other geeks-probably his friends. As if he could see me, I frowned my face and rolled my eyes. He has still been ignoring my text and calls. Whenever we had the same class, he would leave before we were let out. I know he was doing that shit to avoid me. His attitude was starting to get on my fucking nerves.

I sped walked, trying to catch up to Ju. The way he was acting, if saw me, he would probably take off running to avoid me.

"Julius?" I called out. I caught his ass at the top of the steps while he was bending down, tying his shoe. Every time I saw him, he was in a pair of old ass vans or chucks-gosh. His friends were cheesing at me. I ignored them like they weren't there.

He continued to tie his shoe as if I wasn't standing in his face calling his name. I waited impatiently with both hands on my hips. Finally, he stood up, pushing his glasses on his face before giving me his attention. I've always thought he had the prettiest eyes, and the freckles on his nose were cute. He looked from me to his boys.

"I will catch up with you." He said, slapping each one of their hands.

"She's cute." The Steve Urkel look-alike said, giving Ju the thumbs up.

"Yeah, sexy too." The other said, looking like he wanted to take me down.

Ugh.

"Aye, y'all go on." Ju ordered. I caught the stern look on his face. If I didn't know any better, I would say he was feeling a certain way. I smiled; he didn't want his friends lusting over me. When they walked off Ju looked at me, shoving his hands in his pockets.

"What's up, Toya? How you doing?" he gave me the once over; I peeped his approving nod.

"As if you care. How many times have I reached out to you, and you haven't called me back or even responded?"

He laughed.

"What the fuck is so funny?"

"You standing there with your hands on your hips. Head bobbing, looking like a mad chicken."

He put his hands on his waist to mimic me. I didn't want to, but I started laughing, and he joined me.

"Why you always got an attitude?" he asked, hopping down the stairs.

"Why haven't you called me?" I followed behind him, "and why are you walking away while I am talking to you?"

"I got stuff to do, Toya." He tossed over his shoulder.

"Who, that bitch that was on you at the club? You wanna act funny now because you finally getting some pussy."

He halted his steps. One long stride, Ju was in my face—hands gripping both of my wrists.

"You gotta stop coming at me like I am some lame-ass nigga. I am a man, Toya. I may not be one of these punk ass wanna-be thugs you be around here chasing like that shit cute. I'm a man. Respect that or stay the fuck away from me, and I mean that shit ." He growled.

He stared at me for a few seconds before releasing my wrists and walking off. I'm not gonna lie. He had me feeling uneasy. Did I just get checked by

Julius? And did he just exclude himself from being lame? I kissed my teeth and folded my arms across my chest .

"JuJu," I yelled out. Taking a deep breath and blowing it out aggressively. I hoped I didn't have to run after him.

"What girl?" he answered, turning around to face me.

"I'm sorry. Please forgive me for the disrespect. Can we start over?"

"Start what over, woman?" He looked annoyed.

"Being friends. I'm sorry. I got a lot going on, and sometimes I don't think before I speak." I admitted.

It was true. I had a lot going on. My father came to me about getting back in the game. I know he must have thought it out carefully for him to even consider it. After Stormy's mom was killed over a debt he supposedly owed, he gave up on everything. Daddy went downhill. I was the only one who had his back trying to make him remember the man he once was. I wanted my daddy back. He finally had a chance to get his life back on track . Get back to doing what he loved, hustling. The connect wanted 30 g's before they even fucked with him. I had some of the money, but I needed to rush to get the rest. We were 15k short. This shit was stressful.

"JuJu, do you forgive me?" I asked, walking up on him.

He put his hands in his pockets.

"Let me think about it." He stared ahead.

"Juuuuuu," I whined.

"I can't think on an empty stomach, take me to eat." He smirked.

My eyebrows instantly rose; my dad was the only man I spent money on.

"Fine. What are we eating?" I asked.

"You pick."

"I got a taste for tacos, but you know they don't know nothing about good Mexican food out here. Too bad we can't hop on a jet and go to L.A. real quick."

"Right," he said, taking my book bag from me and putting it over his shoulder. "What you got in here?" he asked.

"Books." I laughed.

"Shit heavy."

We walked as I tossed out places to eat. We couldn't agree on anything.

"I got the perfect idea." He offered.

"What's that?" I asked.

"You are about to cook me some tacos."

I couldn't even protest. I wanted tacos . Plus, it would save me some money.

"You heard about that shit that happened in Saint Pete?"

"Nah, what?" he replied, opening my door. I inhaled his sweet cologne lingering in the car. I waited for him to climb into the truck to finish talking.

"It's scary. I don't know how you didn't hear about it. They killed this lady and her dog. But get this, they cut their heads off and placed them on the mantel next to her family photos." I shook my head, "these mutha fuckas are crazy in Florida."

"Wild." He replied, nonchalantly.

"I bet the killer was white, probably her husband. Or some other crazy white person."

"Damn, if you prejudice, just say that."

"I'm not, but us blacks don't do killings like that. We do drive-bys and shit."

"Do I look like a killer to you?" he asked, looking from the road at me.

An eerie feeling came over me; it was the way he said it. I shook my head no.

"And you don't look like you do drive-bys either." He smirked.

But I set niggas up.

Ju turned the radio on full blast. I guess it was his way of shutting me up.

I was shocked by JuJu's choice of music. We bumped Plies and Boosie in his ride. Since it was my date, I thought he would make me pay at the supermarket, but he slid his card. We then went to the liquor bank, and he got a bottle of Patron and Remy with a few chasers. He was doing the most.

"You trying to get me drunk?" I asked.

"Nah, I needed to restock a few items, and since we are in the area, I stopped." He replied casually.

He drove, bobbing his head to Plies. Every now and again, I would feel him look over at me. I caught myself staring at him a few times too. JuJu was cool.

"At Firehouse that night, you didn't wear glasses."

"I broke them, had to get some more, I wore contacts."

"Oh." I simply said, thinking about how he was much cuter without those glasses; it was the grey eyes for me.

"Who lives here?" I asked, eyes big. We were on Treasure Island. Ju looked at me like I asked a dumb question. We pulled into a driveway behind a white Ashton Martin. A BMW motorcycle was also in the driveway. He parked and cut the car off.

"Damn Ju, this how you living?" I asked excitedly.

He looked at me, "Nah, this is my people's house. He out of town." He said flatly.

The house was beautiful inside and out. When I saw the kitchen, I was in heaven.

"I love this kitchen." I cooed.

"It's a kitchen woman."

"If you don't love to cook, you wouldn't understand."

"Oh." He flopped down on a barstool at the counter. "Do your thang. I am going to shower."

"K," I said, taking the things out of the bag.

I whipped the tacos up in no time. On the side were rice and beans and a small salad. JuJu hadn't come back yet. I decided to set the table. When I was done, I took it upon myself to make a drink using the bottle of Patron he purchased. I also thought it'd be cool to give myself a tour around the house. The big ass kitchen was everything. So far, my favorite. I was strolling out of the kitchen, sipping on my drink. I hit the corner and ran into a hard chest. The smell of Axe tickled my nose.

"My bad," he said as I stumbled back, almost spilling my drink.

Got damn, I screamed in my head. Gone were the black funky glasses. Grey eyes glared at me. Red hat to the back. Hard chest covered in ink. Across his six-pack was the word, Dyce. I bit my bottom lip as my eyes zoomed in on his grey sweats. I had to be tripping. There was no way the bulge in his pants was his dick. The transformation had me speechless.

"Are the tacos ready? I'm hungry." He said, stepping around me.

I gulped from my cup.

Julius

I strolled into the kitchen. The expression on Toya's face when she saw me was hilarious. She acts like she saw a whole other nigga. Ain't shit changed about me except what I changed into that made me feel more comfortable in my home. I replaced my glasses for a good reason; I had something in mind, and they could end up broken.

"It smells good up in here. I hope it tastes good." I teased, walking over to the stove.

"I haven't made your shells yet," she said, sounding all timid. "And go wash your hands. Don't you touch nothing."

"I was just looking." I turned and looked at her. I was taking her all in.

Toya was so got damn fine to me. I already knew what her body looked like from seeing her at the strip club. Ashanti was once my biggest crush, but then when Toya came along, she lost her spot. She was standing there looking all bashful and shit but trying her hardest to act like she was unbothered by how good a nigga looked.

"How many?" she asked , looking up at me. The way she was staring into my eyes, she almost made a nigga blush. When her eyes landed on my dick, I chuckled. The girl was staring hard, trying to make sure she wasn't tripping; that was all dick she saw in my grey sweats.

"Are you going to make my tacos, or do I need to help you with your curiosity?" I grabbed the simi hard bulge in my pants and took a few steps toward her.

"You are doing too much, but you know that. "

"How's that?"

"Oh, so you don't know?" she turned the stove burner on and poured a little grape oil in the small pan on top.

"Nah, how am I doing too much?" I walked up behind her, and she tensed up.

"Coming down here trying to look like a thug, showing off your tattoos and stuff."

I gently turned her around to face me. First, I needed to make sure she understood what I was about to explain.

"Ju, why you-"

"Shhh..." I said, putting my finger to my lips. "Listen and listen good, because this will be the last time I explain this to you."

She swallowed the lump in her throat.

"What you see is what you get. I don't have to prove myself to anyone because I am confident in who

I am. My swag may be different from what you consider a fly nigga, but I am that nigga to me. Just because I am white, am smarter than most, and prefer to study than hang around a bunch of fake niggas don't make me a nerd. I do me. I have never had to fake it to make it. So, Toya, whether you see it or not, I am that nigga."

Silence.

"Stop saying that." She whined.

"What?" I asked, seriously.

"Calling yourself a nigga."

"Why?" I questioned .

"It doesn't sound right."

"Don't say that weird shit again. The word nigga doesn't identify a race. To me, nigga ain't no different than saying bro, dude, or homie." I stated matter of factly.

"True," she shrugged. Turning around, she grabbed a tortilla to put in the skillet, but I stopped her. I turned the fire off from under the skillet and pulled her into me. She swallowed the newly formed lump in her throat as I slowly eased toward her lips, placing a light peck on them pretty mutha fuckas. Toya wrapped her arms around my neck. Letting me know that she was on what I was on.

Hungrily I attacked her mouth. Her lips were soft as a marshmallow. I could taste the liquor and pineapple juice on her tongue. Like we have been waiting on this day forever, we feasted on each other's mouths like it was our last supper. Her light moans let me know she was enjoying it. That shit made my dick hard. Effortlessly I picked little momma up; she wrapped her legs around my waist. Our lips never parted as I carried her over to the breakfast nook placing her on top. Toya began to run her hands through my hair. That shit was an orgasm in itself.

Nah, this shit wasn't planned. Well, not in this order. I most definitely had planned on fucking Toya this soon, maybe after dinner. Breaking our kiss, bashfully, she took her bottom lip into her mouth while she stared into my eyes. Placing a kiss on each of her cheeks—another on her nose I never wanted a woman as bad as I wanted Toya.

She placed her hands on my cheeks as she went in for another kiss. Between lip-sucking and tongue dancing, the anticipation was building up.

"Can I, have you ?" I asked; it was a loaded question.

Bottom lip in her mouth, she nodded her head up and down.

"Yes, she wants you." She placed her hands on the crotch of her jeans. "Make her feel good, Ju."

Noted.

"Let's take these off," I said, tugging at her jeans. She lifted her bottom, and I slid them off. Another attack to the mouth as I slid her panties to the side and then slid two fingers into her soaking wet pussy.

"Ohhh shit. Ju. Oh. Oh." She moaned, all sexy and shit.

My mouth watered, thinking about all the shit I would do to her had she given me the correct answer "Yes Ju, you can have me." I'm a freaky nigga. Suck your soul through your pussy, turn you over, and tongue fuck you in the ass type nigga. But, then, just when you think you couldn't take it anymore, I'm a black bag full of tricks ass freak. Toya and I weren't on that, though. Although, we probably didn't need to be.

She tugged at my sweats until her hand was inside. She gripped my shit.

"Damn Ju." She moaned, pulling it out; her eyes bulged when she saw what she was holding .

"How long you going to look at it?"

Taking my shit back from her, I watched her closely, and teased her by rubbing the head of my dick up and down her center; gushing sounds and moans filled the air. No introduction was needed; I rammed myself into her. We both moaned. I paused. I was savoring the moment before I explored her walls.

"So fucking wet and tight, Toya."

"Juuuuuu... damn. You feel so good inside of me." She squealed, head back, mouth open. Then, I buried my head in the crook of her neck as I deep stroked her into the orgasm of her life. Toya had me stopping every few seconds. I wasn't trying to bust. She was putting it on me. I felt like she was trying to make me fall for her more than I already was. It was working too.

"Toyaaaaa. Fuck."

"Juuuui babe it's so good. What you doing to me." Her body began to shake.

I planned on being inside her all night.

Toya

Lying next to him as he slept, I couldn't believe I had given it up to him. Ju wasn't my type at all. You couldn't have paid me to believe I would give it up to a guy I considered a nerdy white boy and without getting his bread at that. This time felt different tho. I thought about what Crystal said that day at the Firehouse, about how Ju has a big one. He definitely knew how to use it, that shit was for sure, but who else was he fucking around campus for her to know? Whoever it was, I bet their pussy wasn't as wet and tight as mine. Bet my shit make him forget whoever the bitch was. He sure surprised me. He took my body places she ain't ever been. The boy had me speaking in tongues and I wasn't ashamed either. I peeped how he didn't eat my pussy. Eating the pussy was a rule of mine before I gave it up but the dick had me not worried about what that tongue do. I know he wasn't expecting me to gulp that dick down my throat. He acted like he was about to have a seizure when I sucked his seeds out. Three rounds and each one got better and better. We fell asleep in the most awkward position.

Easing out of the bed, I made my way to the restroom to wash up before going back downstairs into the kitchen, where I left my phone. I saw had a few missed calls from my dad. I didn't bother to call back. I told him I would get the money. I hated when he worried. It stressed me. Stormy called too. I smiled, ready to tell her all about what the fuck had just gone down with me.

"Hello," I said, answering my vibrating phone. It was my twin. He was calling me on FaceTime audio.

"Hey, girl." He said.

"Hey, boo."

"We be out there this weekend."

"I thought you said next month."

"We coming on business. If the play we been working on come through, we set for a long ass time."

"Who is it?"

"I'll tell you when I get there."

I haven't helped my brothers set anyone up in a couple of years. This would be right on time. I needed the money, and until I got it, I was still going to hustle.

I made my way back to the bedroom. Ju was still sleeping. I smiled as I passed by him into the bathroom.

"Ju," I called out, coming from his bathroom. I hated to bother him. He was comatose after all that fucking, we did. After the quickie in the kitchen, we ate and then fucked some more. I wouldn't mind snuggling next to him, but I had money to make. "Ju," I repeated a little louder.

"Yeah," he grumbled.

"I need to get home. I have something to do."

Eyes closed, he inhaled, exhaled, then he jumped up from the bed.

"Let me take a shower first," he sounded like he had an attitude.

"Ju. There's a new club that just opened in Saint Pete. My roommate told me it's amateur night. I need to get there. Otherwise, I wouldn't have woken you up. I would've taken an Uber when I was ready."

The way he was staring at me made me feel uneasy; I looked down at the carpet.

"I'll be downstairs," I said, walking out.

I was in the kitchen having a drink when Ju walked in. I rolled my eyes, seeing that he had his glasses on, skinny jeans, black T and vans. Gone was the sexy thugged out white boy with the big dick.

"You ready?" He asked, attitude still evident.

" Ju, I was wondering if you could take me to my place, wait while I change, and come with me. It's a new place, and you know." I shrugged, looking at him with hopeful eyes. Shit, maybe afterward we could come back and chill.

Ding... Dong... The doorbell chimed.

He left me in the kitchen to answer the door.

"Hey. Are you leaving?" I heard a chick's voice. "Did you forget we had a date?"

I walked up out of that kitchen so quick. Standing in the house was a Becky. White girl with glasses and two ponytails. She wore leggings, a tank top, and a varsity jacket.

"I brought you food. Oh, and if you can help me with the bags in my truck. I got the stuff to decorate your downstairs bathroom and I also got you a few groceries so you can stop eating out." Finally, she looked up and saw me,

"I didn't know you had company,"

"Girl, I'm about to leave. Just waiting on my Uber." I couldn't do shit but chuckle.

It was very amusing.

Julius

"Amber, take the food in the kitchen. Toya, already cooked tacos." I said, trying to figure out how I was going to explain this shit.

"Oh, she cooked?" she retorted as if she was feeling some kind of way.

"Amber," Toya chuckled while messing around on her phone, probably calling an Uber.

"Amber Rose Charleston. I am named after my great-grandmother. A famous model from London." Amber stated. She was always with the extras when it came to letting people know she was a generational rich kid.

"Girl, I don't care," Toya said, walking out the front door. She was mad. I hoped she didn't flip out. My head hurt just thinking about her tripping.

I looked at Amber,

"I am about to go somewhere with Toya. Don't wait up. And don't go to my room. We can chill in the guest room tonight."

"Why can't I go into your room?" Amber asked, looking from me to Toya.

Toya's head turned around so quick it was a surprise her neck didn't snap. Her sharp glare was on Amber, giving her the once over, and then she looked at me.

"Julius, I am good. My Uber is on the way. Thanks anyway." She forced a smile.

I rubbed my hand down my face in hopes of relieving some stress. I know Toya was pissed. She gave up the pussy and shortly after I got another female popping up at my house with food and shit to decorate my bathroom. Amber was feeling some kind of way, but she wouldn't address it until we were alone. But on some real shit, I didn't owe any of them an explanation. Especially not Toya. She didn't want me her ego was just bruised.

"Look, I'm taking you home and to the other place you asked me to take you. We already agreed to do this, so I ain't sure why you changed your mind all of a sudden." I furrowed my eyebrows and she just stared at me.

" I was being polite since you have company. But, if you and Amber don't mind neither do I. Let's go." She walked toward the driveway, and I followed suit.

"Julius, should I wash your covers?" Amber called out trying to be funny, but I ignored her. Surprisingly Toya did too.

I hadn't put gas in the truck, so I was taking the Ashton Martin.

"We taking this car," I called out to Toya, who was headed toward the truck. I waited for her with the door open and after she climbed in, I shut it. Toya had me feeling like I was in trouble, like I had to explain myself. A nigga heart was beating a little too fast for my liking. This girl did something to me. The fight to shake her was going to be hard.

"So, is this your car or the people who live here?" she chuckled. " I hope they like the way Amber decorates."

"Ain't my house, ain't my car." I lied again, knowing the shit was going to catch up with me. It didn't matter because she ain't my girl.

I sat in front of Toya's place for a good hour. I was starting to think she was making me wait on purpose. Strutting toward the car in a black maxi dress with her bag over her shoulder she looked so good to me. Knowing the scowl on her face was because of me tugged at my heart. Desperately I wanted to hop out the car, pull her into my arms and ask her to forgive me. BUT FOR WHAT?

"You smell good, what you wearing, Chanel?" I asked when she got in.

"Yeah." She said, messing with her phone. Her fingers were going a mile a minute. I wondered if she was talking about me. I pulled off.

"Where you going?" she asked looking up from her phone.

"To the club."

"But I didn't tell you where it was at."

That was true. All she said was the name. I knew what she was talking about because I was the secret owner.

"You told me the name, Toya."

"Yeah, you probably know where all the spots are Mr. Get Around."

I didn't even bother to bite into that. She was mad and she had a right to feel the way she felt.

YG played for the next thirty minutes. We pulled into the clubs' lot and I smiled. The blue Dyce sign on the side of the black building looked good. I had a dude come out and paint it yesterday, it was my first time seeing it.

"That says reserved." She said when I pulled into my parking spot. Of course, Toya had no idea it was my spot.

"What they going to do, tow my shit?" I played it off like I didn't care.

While I was waiting on her to change , I already told them niggas she wasn't for hire . So, she could dance tonight and make a little money, but she wouldn't be working there and that's on me. Picking up my phone I texted my general manager to let him know we were about to come in.

"Thanks for the ride. You don't have to wait; I got a ride home."

"Who?" I snapped, ready to go off. I had to calm down because we wasn't even on that.

"No one important to you. He got me, Ju. Thanks for always having my back. I know you don't have to." She said kissing me on the cheek.

I wasn't used to the feeling I was having thinking that this would be the last time Toya and I connected on the level we shared at the house. I was scared to lose her.

I grabbed her before she could get out my car.

"Ju, I gotta go."

"Amber isn't my girl," I confessed.

With a blank expression, she stared into my eyes.

" Aww." She started. "You guys make a cute couple. If you feel you owe me an explanation you don't. We fucked. You are not my man and I'm not your girl. I don't care one way or the other." She shrugged. "See you around Julius." She climbed out the car and politely shut the door. As she crossed the front of the car, she waved bye to me. It was the fake ass smile that told me how she really felt. Toya wasn't fucking with me anymore. She felt played.

I'll give her some space. My jaws tightened thinking about what she and that nigga who escorted her in the club would probably get into later.

Stormy

When the jet landed, I was waking up again from another nap. After two tequila shots and a Tylenol PM, I slept on and off the entire trip. Blake had pissed me off, so got damn bad putting my business out there like that. I wanted to avoid him at all costs. When I got up to go to the restroom, he tried to come behind me, whispering a weak-ass apology. I gave his pale ass the death stare. His pink ass was quick to get out of my face. He knew got damn well that was a forbidden subject for me. He knew that part of my life I wanted to forget about. In my opinion, I had no father. My father's dealings in the drug game are why my mom is dead. For him to say that was some straight bitch shit. I'm sure I wouldn't avoid him the entire four days on the island, but I wouldn't talk to his ass until I felt like it.

The pilot announced our arrival. I looked out the window; the water was breath taking, a beautiful turquoise blue. You could see right through the ocean. Sadly, Blake and I have only been out of the country twice our entire relationship, and neither time compared to this.

Rising from my seat , I pulled my glasses from the top of my head and slid them over my eyes. My blood pressure began to rise when Blake approached me. I stared straight ahead.

"Baby. Let's have ourselves a good time. Whatever issues we have with each other, we will discuss them at home."

So, his clear ass told me to forget what he said and enjoy my time with him. I walked right past him and waited my turn to exit the jet.

"Fine, if that's how you wanna be." I was seconds away from spazzing on him, but I held my cool. Blake could kiss my ass.

My eyes kept glancing toward the direction Dyce walked in. I don't know why I was nervous, but I was. Maybe it was how he unapologetically stared at me with lust-filled eyes and didn't care who was watching. Or how I allowed him to bully me into taking off my shades. He spoke, and I followed his command. Very intriguing, he was darkness. Danger. Power. No nonsense oozed from his pores. Not that I was interested, but I planned to stay far away from him.

It was finally my turn to exit. Talk about clear blue skies. Even the air smelled fresh. The scenery was green and clean. Three Hummer limos awaited us. Mrs. Whitman was standing by one of them. When she saw me, she waved me over . I was glad Blake didn't ride with us, but I was also pissed he didn't attempt to. I was upset with him but had he got in the same vehicle with Jamie, I would've gone in on his ass. Between my thoughts and enjoying the scenery, I was quiet the entire ride.

Finally, we arrived at the resort. I wondered if heaven was this beautiful. I looked across the way, there he was, Dyce. He was standing by one of the Hummers talking to the driver—no emotion on his face. The man was mean.

We were escorted to where we would be staying by the host- Pure Luxury. There was enough room so Blake and I could have our own space. He went to shower, and I went to get fresh air.

I walked onto the balcony. A bottle of champagne in ice sat on the table. I poured myself a glass and stood over the rail. I stared into the ocean, enjoying the ocean's sounds and the cool breeze just chilling in my own world.

"You wanna be mad the entire vacation that's on you. I'm going to have a good time."

I didn't bother to acknowledge Blake. Instead, I sipped from my flute as if he wasn't there. He eventually left back out, and that was fine with me.

I relaxed on the balcony for a good while dang near drinking a full bottle of champagne. I demolished the fruit tray that was set out also. I was tipsy as hell and the fruit hadn't done anything to soak up the alcohol in my system. Deciding that I would go out I headed for the room. I gathered my things from my suitcase and went and took a hot shower. I thought of Blake and frowned. "Selfish bitch." I growled. It's been two hours and he hadn't sent a text or anything to check on me. When Mr. Lloyd Dyce crossed my mind the girl between my legs began to throb. Blame it on the liquor because if I wasn't half drunk there would be no way I would be imagining that man's head between my legs. Just because I did not date black men didn't mean I didn't know what a fine man looked like. Nasty thoughts of Lloyd and the things he could do with his tongue had me so got damn wet. I slid my hand down my clit and my finger into my dripping wet hole. A master at pleasing myself I came hard. Whew! I was waiting on guilt to wash over me but there was nothing. It felt so good I was tempted to go a second round. Two orgasms later, I was dressed in a white sheer baby doll dress. Checked my phone and there was still nothing from Blake. My feelings were a little hurt.

---"You never said thank you for the flowers." The deep baritone startled me.

"Oh my god," I screamed, "oh my god." My heart was beating fast. The asshole sitting on the sofa scared the shit out of me. "What the hell are you doing breaking in here?" I screamed looking at the door and back at him. Dressed in all black he sat staring at me.

"The door was unlocked. But I would've come in any way."

"Why? What the fuck? What right do you have coming in here?"

He smirked. Eyeing me like I was a full course meal , when he stood up, I wasn't scared, I was more so wondering what he would do to me.

"Why are you here?" I asked.

He hovered over me looking down into my eyes as if he was trying to hypnotize me.

"I gave you flowers. Why didn't you call me to say thank you?"

When I decided not to call him, I knew exactly why. I didn't ask for the flowers. I didn't want them. And I wasn't interested in him, there was no need to say anything. Now as I stand here looking up at this tall dark man, I couldn't tell the truth.

"Thank you. Can you leave before my man comes?" I looked at the door.

"Yeah, let's go." He ordered.

"What, no." I replied. I wasn't going anywhere with that man.

"Let's go Stormy or do you prefer we hang out here?" He asked looking around the front room. Of course, I didn't want to hang out here or anywhere else.

If Blake walked in that door and saw us all hell would break loose. If people saw us together, it'll be some shit.

"Let's go." I said scurrying to and out the door.

"Relax Stormy. Michelle took them all on a tour." I looked back at him.

"Look, I'm not sure what you got on your mind but I'm not it. I'm a mar-. I'm in a relationship. And you're in a relationship. Even if you weren't I wouldn't be interested."

I looked back at him again he had his hands in his pockets strolling up behind me wearing a smirk.

"I'm glad you find this funny."

"This way." He said. I looked up at him, he tilted his head toward the Hummer.

I don't know what the hell got into me, but I went with him.

"You smell good Stormy." I could feel his gaze on me.

I parted my lips to respond but my tummy spoke first.

"Humph. You're hungry." He acknowledged.

I could've cussed my stomach out. 'I was going to feed your ass; you didn't have to do all that.' I went off in my head.

Lloyd began to talk to the driver in another language.

"You have a problem with thank you?"

"What?"

"I said you smell good."

"Thank you."

"May I," I reached over to grab the bottle of tequila from the ice bucket. Lloyd placed his hand on top of mine. Butterflies took over the hunger pains and between my legs began to throb. Looking over at me his hooded eyes bored into my soul.

"You need to eat first. Almost there."

"You're right." I tried to pull my hand away, but he didn't move his.

"You're beautiful. A very beautiful black queen."

"Thank you." I blushed.

"Ohhh. You caught on," he smiled displaying a set of perfect white teeth.

I giggled.

"How did you get the name Stormy, and the mole?" His eyes zoomed in on my mouth staring at the cloud on my lower lip.

"It's a birthmark, not a mole," I answered. Whenever I thought about my mother my heart was saddened. It's been eleven years and it still hurts like it was yesterday. I took a deep breath and let it out. "My mother named me. She said I am a reminder that Storms don't last forever. When she was pregnant with me, she was going through a lot. The biggest one was her mother disowning her." I glanced at him, " She forbade my mother from dating my father. He was bad news. A drug dealer who couldn't promise her nothing but misery." Gawking at Lloyd I could see his expression never wavered. In fact, I think I saw sadness in his eyes. "And she was right. Caused me misery too." I added.

"You are her reminder that no manner how hard it may seem, there is a beautiful blessing in every lesson."

"I was her reminder. And yes."

" I wanna kiss that birthmark one day," he stated boldly.

"Are you serious?" My brows rose . "We shouldn't even be together right now. We are both taken ."

"I am very serious. I'm patient though." He turned and faced forward sitting back in his seat. He then took my hand into his.

"Blake, why are you with him? What is the reason? And don't tell me attraction. I wanna know your story."

"What do you mean?"

"Women like you don't just fall for men like Blake Whitman."

"Women like me?" I snapped.

"Settle down pretty face. Jumping to conclusions is never good. It always almost turns into the other person being made a fool."

"Wow." I tried to pull my hand away, but he wouldn't let go. Lloyd continued to overstep his boundaries and I allowed him to.

"You said your mother fell for a drug dealer. I would like to assume she stayed with him. You are well-spoken but I pick up on your slang. You dress stylish but touch it up with sexiness and class. I peeped that the three times I saw you dressed. You ordered tequila shots and, on the jet, you went for Hennessy. You left the hood to find yourself. You wanted more than where you come from. Tell me, why did you choose Blake?"

Consider me read. Was it that obvious that I was a ghetto girl running from her past caught up in a fantasy world? Maybe that's why Mr. Whitman didn't like me. Maybe he thought I was using his son for gain, and not that I loved him.

"Where are you from Stormy?"

"Orange County."

"Where did you grow up?"

"That doesn't matter. Why are you with the Asian chick? Are you running from something?"

"I don't run. I stand ten toes down. I will never run out on those I love. I will never run from my past. I take responsibility and own up to everything. I have to. I will be a coward if I don't." He spoke with anger, his hazel eyes turned black. Whatever emotion I woke up inside him bothered him a lot. I squeezed his hand, one to let him know it was ok, and two to bring him back to his peace.

"Are we ever going to eat?" I asked, changing the subject. Plus, I was hungry.

"We are here now pretty face." He said and the car slowed down.

I looked out the window. We were in the middle of the island and from what I could see nothing else was around us.

"I'll never hurt you." He lifted my hand and kissed it. "This is my private island. You are the first lady I brought here. No one else has been here besides my brothers."

"Wow. Not even Jamie?"

"I don't lie Stormy; I know the truth can hurt but it's the best way. AND to answer your question about Jaime. It's business. I don't love her and never will."

I don't know what kind of business deal he had going on and I didn't want to know. My next question was the biggest one of all. I refrained from asking for fear of sounding judgmental and being made to look like a fool .

Lloyd's door opened and he stepped out. As I waited for him to open my door, I looked at my cellphone and noticed Blake hadn't reached out not once. My blood began to boil. With Lloyd telling me he and his woman was business and how he didn't love her had me thinking. Jamie had been flirting with my man. Were they together? Was this part of their plan?

"Stop thinking so much." Lloyd said, holding my door open. I looked up at him wondering if there was a motive. He grabbed my hand and I climbed out of the car. My mouth dropped. There was a tent with clear lights around it. Under the tent was an entire buffet . Two chefs awaited us. Who in the hell is this man? And why was he going out of his way to make me feel special?

"Thank you, it's amazing," I said.

Later...

"Everything was amazing. The food is delicious. I feel so guilty but if I had enough room I would eat more." I admitted.

Lloyd was escorting me to his villa. "I need to release my bladder."

"Thank you for coming." He replied.

His comment made me think about my actions. I shouldn't have come. This is cheating.

"I can't do this again. Thank you but this wasn't right. I love my man." I stopped and looked at him." Despite what it may seem like, I love Blake. He has his ways and can piss me off to the point where I want to kill him, but I love him enough to know that no man is perfect. Rich, poor, white, or black."

"I thought you had to use the restroom." He said, changing the subject. Lloyd led me inside and I used the restroom. When I came back out, he had a glass of cognac in his hand extending it to me.

"Thank you." I took a sip.

"You're welcome." He took a sip from his glass.

I followed him out the door, he led me to the swings. We both took a seat.

"Stormy." My name rolled off his tongue. His eyes were on the moon.

We sat for a while in our thoughts. I was the first to break the silence.

"I left my city when I was eighteen. After my mother died. I went into a depression. A year later I got myself together. Left Cali and went to New York for

159

college. College is where I ran into Blake for the second time. The first time was at Target." I smiled. "I was in a bad mood missing my mom. I went out in the rain to get fresh air. I ran into Blake when I was browsing the book section. We both were looking for a good urban fiction book. We exchanged numbers. I enjoyed the times we talked but when I found out he was the son of a famous attorney I shut down. I guess because I was embarrassed by where I had come from. The daughter of a drug dealer isn't something to be proud of. Maybe in the hood." I shrugged. "Disappointed that I was born into a life I wanted no parts of. I stopped answering his calls. One year later, I ran into him in college. And we have been together ever since. His father hates he's with me. Blake doesn't care. He loves me," I smiled softly.

"What was your major?" Lloyd asked.

I chuckled. Fine, he didn't have to give a shit.

"Dance."

"That's dope. A dancer." He eyed me.

"Yes. Soon I'll be opening up my own studio."

"Hell yeah. The calm after the storm,"

"What?"

"I think you should call your studios the calm after the storm. You're going to open them all over the country right?"

"Yeah, I am." I smiled.

"That's what's up. Yeah. The world will know your name."

"They will." I nodded proudly.

Lloyd took my hand and looked at me. I gazed into those beautiful eyes.

"Never be ashamed of where you come from. Your story is your story, a mutha fucka can't respect that that's their problem. Always be you. The best version of you."

I simply responded with a warm smile.

His phone rang. I tried to peep at who was calling, figuring maybe it was Jamie; we've been gone for a long time. I got nervous thinking about what Blake was probably thinking if he was back and I wasn't there.

"What's up bro?" he answered,

He stood from the swing and walked away. I decided to use that time to call Blake. His phone went straight to voicemail. Anxiety washed over me. I called Mrs. Whitman. She told me she wasn't with him. And to call Michelle. Before I could tell her I didn't have her number, she hung up. Right after that, I received a text from her. I then called Michelle.

"This is Michelle."

"Hi, it's Stormy. Is Blake with you?"

"Yes. He's up front." She replied flatly, "we're almost there. Enjoy yourself." She replied and hung up.

" Stormy sweetheart." Lloyd's voice pulled me from my sudden trance. "I have to fly back home. Family emergency. My driver will take you back."

"Oh ok."

"I had a good time." He pulled me into his arms. " I'll never hurt you. Don't be so nervous." Lloyd leaned down and kissed me on the corner of my mouth before licking my entire lip.

I was blown. My kitty was crying out. Whatever spell this man was putting on me was working. I wanted him and I knew the shit was wrong. Smoothly, he slipped his fingers under my dress and pulled my panties to the side. I gasped when he slipped a finger into my dripping wet center and then another. I was definitely under his spell. He covered my mouth with his and pleasured me until my juices flowed.

"Thank you," he whispered. Lloyd eased his hand out of me and placed his sticky fingers on my lips. One by one I sucked my juices off.

Looking into those grey eyes I was hoping he would take what I knew he wanted, what I desired but instead he pulled away.

"Until next time." He smiled. "Go."

Although disappointed I had to go. Though I walked away with my head high I was ashamed of my actions. But damn, I'll never forget him.

Lloyd

The phone call I received was about more bullshit. Niggas was steady coming for us, I assume, with intentions of taking over. That wasn't going to happen. All they were doing was making us mad. The Dyce brothers were no weak links. The entire city was about to be a blood bath fucking with us. We'd be some bitch as niggas if we sat back and let a mutha fucka steal what's ours. It was time for Dark Vader to come out of retirement. I hope they know I wouldn't sleep until they all were dead.

Although the phone call fucked up my mind, I needed the distraction. I have never wanted a woman as bad as I wanted her in all my life. The first time I laid eyes on Stormy, I thought she was beautiful enough to fuck. When Ross told me about her choice not to date her race, I wanted to punish her for such foolishness. But, instead, I found myself thinking about and lusting after her, wondering who hurt her, sending her flowers, and checking my phone to see if she would call to say thank you. Not knowing much about her, I still felt like she was who I needed in my life. But I had Jamie. I didn't want her, but I had her. Plus, Stormy wouldn't accept me. I couldn't give her what she desired. No matter how much money I have, what I drove, or the fact that I own millions in real estate, Lloyd Dyce is a street nigga. A street nigga is who she wanted no parts of. Do I think I had what it took to make her accept me? Damn, right, I do. But I respected her too much to take it there with her.

I couldn't leave Jamie. Her family and my family will be forever bonded. And I owe her me even if my heart is begging to leave.

Jamie is the daughter of Mr. Cheng. Cheng is one of the biggest crooks in China. He is so powerful that he never has to step foot in America; he has several crews in different parts of California. All he has to do is make one phone call, and that is your ass. The drugs my parents came up on belonged to one of Cheng's men. He was in the UK trying to set up shop when he got hit by my mother. My mom took every brick he had, and my father killed him. Not knowing who they robbed, they fled to America. Within a year, Cheng located them. They never knew how. Cheng demanded his drugs back or they had to triple the money owed. So, to pay off the debt, they worked for him. Eventually, he became their connect. I was fifteen when Cheng sent my father and his oldest son to come to China. While my father was talking business, I was fucking on a six-teen-year-old Li jing "Jamie" Cheng.

She became pregnant, and her father beat her so bad she lost the baby. He treated her like shit from that point forward. He also wanted the person's head who was fucking his daughter, and she refused to snitch. Cheng disowned her. Her mother's brother, who also worked for Cheng carried Jamie to the states where he would make a new life. My parents began to work under him. By the time I saw Jamie again she was

Americanized. She was one of the hottest Asian chicks I have ever seen. We began to sneak around. Jamie fell in love, but I was out in the streets doing me. I left for college. I learned Jamie went back to China for her mother's funeral. She was gone for two years and when she returned my father told me I was to marry her. I tripped. That was the first time I have ever blown up on my pops but when he explained why- I had no choice but to obey . Besides Jamie, there are only three of us that know what she did to save Dyce.

Jamie knew I didn't love her, she believed her loving me was enough. It wasn't but I had to do what I promised I would do.

Just like I had to do what I had to do back in Fiji. I put laxative in Jamie's food to keep her inside. I paid Michelle's crazy-ass 10k to take Blake and the others on a tour that would leave them occupied for hours. I wanted to be with Stormy with no distractions and it worked. I saw the disappointment on her face when I told her I had to leave. I also, peeped how she tried to hold her head up high and walk away with pride. She wanted me just as much as I needed her.

Once on the jet, I called up Michelle to let her know I was leaving. I then ordered her to go and check on Stormy. Just incase Blake was on some fuck boy shit.

"What happened between y'all?" she quizzed.

"Why?"

"Because that is my-. Stormy is a woman who has been through enough and I hate to see her go

165

through anything else." She sighed. "I should have never taken the bribe."

"But you did. " I replied firmly. "I won't hurt her. She is good. Whatever started has ended. Go check on her."

"Will do."

With that, we ended our call. When I closed my eyes, I thought of Stormy. It was then that I knew walking away from what we could potentially have would be hard.

Stormy

"Hello, is anyone in here?" The voice was faint near the front door. "Hello?" She announced again.

Lying on the livingroom floor, I balled up into a fetal position and cried. I was afraid to move. I was scared that the man I loved would hurt me again.

"Oh my god baby, what's wrong?" I heard Michelle's voice.

Too ashamed to share my truth, I didn't acknowledge her.

"Was it Blake did he hurt you? What did he do?" She sat on the floor beside me, rubbing my back. "Where is he, is he here?" Her voice rose , I could detect both anger and concern in her tone.

"I just wanna leave." I cried finally sitting up.

Michelle's gaze was filled with worry . Her eyebrows suddenly furrowed. My mom's left eye would jump like that when she was upset. I guess it was the black woman's signature look when upset because I've seen my mom with the same facial expression when she went off on one of my teachers.

"Ok. I'll handle it." She said. "Let's go get you washed up. You look a mess." She added.

Just when I thought she was being nice.

"That mutha fucka messing with the wrong one." She mumbled. I don't know when Michelle became a fan of mine, but I appreciated her concern.

I gasped at what I saw when I looked in the mirror. Scratches were on my neck, and face. I lost my mind. Yes me. I was so busy trying to calm him down that I allowed him to hurt me. I should've fucked his ass up.

**

When I walked into the villa, I was expecting to see Blake sitting in the living area waiting to scold me. After searching the entire hut there was no sign of Blake. My overthinking disorder kicked in and I began to become suspicious. Was Lloyd and Michelle working together to get me away from Blake so he and Jaimie could be together? Taking a deep breath, I flopped down on the sofa. Contemplating if I should reach out to Blake or not. Crossing my right leg over the other I began to shake my foot. If Blake was cheating, I would flip. I swear he didn't want to see that side of me. I've popped off on his ass over the years, but I never showed him how I could really get down.

I wasn't going to call looking for him again, I'll wait.

I stood up from the sofa to head to the shower. Blake came storming through the door. Immediately, fear took over and I was scared to know what it was that he was mad about and what he would do to me. My eyes zoomed in on him; I could tell that he was drunk. His blue eyes were glossy. The closer he drew, I was able to get a whiff of him, and he smelled like he drank an entire bottle of whisky.

"Is everything ok?" I asked.

"No. How can it be when my wife is acting like a stuck-up bitch." He yelled.

I was shocked by his outburst for a minute. Blake had lost his mind. Now, all of a sudden, he wanted to acknowledge I'm his wife.

"Who in the fuck are you talking to like that?"

"You. I brought you out here to show you something different." He growled, spit flying from his mouth.

"First off, I told you to cancel. You didn't pay for the trip anyway."

"And neither did you. Look. I'm not about to argue with your ungrateful ass. Let's go shower. I need sex."

"I am not having sex with you?" The hell he thought he was talking to.

"I'm your got damn husband."

"All of a sudden? I have been your wife for two years mutha fucka. That doesn't mean shit to you. We don't even fucking live together. Too worried about what your father would say. You know what. I'm tired of living a secret life. I did that before and how I got tricked into doing it again I don't know. But this is it!" I yelled, face full of tears.

"Stormy, I don't need you. If you wanna go. Go."

"Really?"

"Just shut up with all that. You are too emotional. I'm asking my wife for sex, and you can't do that? Worthless."

Wham.

I slapped Blake and he attacked me. Grabbing me by the neck and throwing me to the floor hitting me. I begged him to calm

down. For us to talk about it. He wouldn't listen. After putting his hands on me he raped me.

I showered and changed. When I walked back into the living room Michelle was still there. Her legs were crossed with a joint in her hand. This woman.

"Are you ok?" she asked me.

"Yes," I replied somberly. "I spoke with a friend. He says that he can get you out tomorrow. I think we should all go." Michelle said.

"I don't want people in my business."

"We will say you are sick. Besides, Jamie still has a stomach virus."

"She didn't go with you guys?"

"No. She was very sick." She looked down at the floor.

"Thank you for arranging for me to get out of here."

"No problem. I hope you don't hit back."

" Look, I don't need you in my business. If accepting your help makes you think you have a right to speak up on something that has nothing to do with you then you can leave. I'll find my own way home."

"Stormy. I know more than you think I do. So does his mother."

"Ok. I'm grown." I snapped.

"You're also a smart and beautiful woman who's losing herself for a fiction love. Here." She extended her hand out.

"What's that?" I looked at the object she was holding .

"I found his phone by the sofa. I'm sure he's looking for it, hopefully you have the password. Maybe there's something in there that will give you the courage to let this go."

She stood up, gave me a pitying look, and left.

2 days later...

"What in the fuck are you doing at my house? Does Blake know that you are here?" The woman who was stored in my husband's phone as wifey yelled at me. She looked at me like I was the scum of the fucking earth. It was obvious she knew who I was from her reaction. I damn sure didn't know shit about her until Michelle gave me Blake's phone. I almost hate that I even looked through his phone. Fear of what I may find out had me hesitant. It wasn't until I was on the jet the following day without so much as a word from Blake that I decided to scroll. The most recent text was between him and his father.

Father: UNBELIEVABLE. I will not get you out of this one. ARE you FUCKING kidding me?? I am removing you from everything. Divorce that got damn ghetto gold digger before I die.

Father: Does your mother know about this?

I continued to read through the thread. That's when I learned how Blake really felt about me. His father shared with him how he spent time with his grandson. Initially, I wondered who? Did Blake have siblings I didn't know about? The next message clarified everything.

Father: You should be ashamed. How long will you keep your child a secret to please her. End it with her and be with your family.

I gasped, looking around as if someone was about to jump out and reveal that this was all a prank. I had to read it again, and again to make sure I wasn't imagining things. Blake's punk ass going to say.

Blake: I want to be with my son. I want to marry his mom. I screwed up dad.

Father: How Blake?

Father: I married Stormy after college. No prenup. I'm sorry.

Ohhhh, so that's how he found out. Blake texted first crying like a hoe.

With my free hand, I covered my mouth as if our marriage had just been revealed to me as well. It's true. Blake and I eloped right after college. We got married in Las Vegas. That was almost two years ago. And as embarrassed as I am to admit it he told me that we need to keep it a secret and I did. I agreed to hide our marriage until he said it was OK. Years have passed and I'm waiting for the man I love, the man that I married to announce to his family that we are husband and wife. Almost two years I waited to have this fantasy wedding he promised me we would have. Here I was, going through the same shit I did with Deon. I was done. I was done with Blake after reading

172

the messages . I didn't want his white ass any fucking more. Fuck Blake Whitman!! I didn't wanna know why he did it and I wasn't gonna beg him to stay with me. In my heart, I knew I was completely done. And the only reason why I showed up at this bitch's house is that I had to see.

She'd told him that he needed to get back to her or she was packing up their kid and leaving to be with her mother. I took that as a sign that I was supposed to show up at that bitch's door and personally deliver a message. Of course, her address was saved under her contact information.

Standing at her front door in a daze, I couldn't even respond. I was numb. Reading the text and actually seeing this woman holding my husband's child took my breath away. A fucking newborn. Wow!!

"Why the fuck are you here?" She yelled and the baby began to cry.

"Fuck this," I said turning to walk off. I knew the truth. I read the messages. I shouldn't have come. It was a stupid move I made off emotions.

"You shouldn't have come in the first place. He doesn't love you. Give him the divorce. Gold digger."

I stopped in my tracks. A gold-digger is what his fucking father called me and I assume Blake may have been saying the same fucking thing. My husband talked about me to this bitch.

I was fucking angry. I stomped back up the stairs and she stood there boldly. Her expression was smug.

"What the fuck are you going to do? He doesn't love you. You're so stupid and desperate." She sneered.

"Bitch I'm not desperate, you are and that's why you are fucking a man you know is married. I am a gold digger. Yup." I laughed. "And that's why I will never divorce my husband. You think I am going to allow you to take my money? Fuck you and that bastard child." I bellowed.

"Black bitch." She sneered.

I laughed ready to fire back until that bitch spit in my face.

I lost it. Before I knew it, I drew my hand back and punched that hoe in the face.

"Ahhhh!" She screamed, dropping the baby from her grip.

"Help, call the police. She attacked me." She screamed. Her cries weren't as loud as the baby's.

I drew my fist back and punched that hoe again. Something was telling me to stop. Get in my car and leave but anger overtook being rational. I grabbed her by the hair holding her head down and used my free hand to uppercut her. I had no plans of stopping. I was going to beat her ass so bad she would remember me every day of her life.

"Help. Stop!" She screamed louder.

"You talked all that shit. Take this." I continued to punch her.

I lifted my hand to swing again but the powerful blow to the back of my head dazed me. The second blow caused me to grab my head and then everything went black.

Toya

Me and my brother were at the mall in the food court eating Panda. Our big brother ended up going to jail. The nigga couldn't keep his hands off his boyfriend. He was the most insecure fine nigga I knew. Nobody wanted that big black gremlin but him. Now, don't get me wrong, Iso is cool but he still ugly as hell.

"What's on your mind sis?" My twin asked.

Travis put you in the mind of the rapper Nip. Except he only had one chain and didn't bang. My brother was fine.

"Thinking about this move, hope we can pull it off without bro." I said telling only half of what I was thinking.

I was also thinking about how good this damn food was and how I wanted to take some home for later.

By the way, I didn't get hired at the new club and that's been on my mind too. Them bitches knew I was the baddest one in there. My talent was unmatched. Somebody was hating because ain't no way I didn't make the cut. I needed this lick.

"This shit going to be easy. I just found out some shit." Twin announced.

I looked up at him.

"What and is the source reliable?"

"Yeah. Very." He said staring into a daze.

"Somebody trying to send them a message."

"Deon got out. Now all of a sudden the nigga Bishop and a few other trap spots been robbed." He reveals. "Sounds fishy to me."

"Fuck no. When?" I asked.

"Nigga. No lie. The other day they say. So, when we rob Bishop, they are going to think it's Deon or whoever hit them the first time." He shrugged.

I sat thinking about whether I wanted to go through with this or not. Bishop was cool. Anytime I asked he gave. I didn't have a reason to do him like that.

"Look sis. Just remember it ain't him you taking from, it's his boss. Them niggas paid."

"Who's the boss? How dangerous are they?"

He fanned his hand.

"They across the country somewhere. They don't handle small shit like this. You been messing with dude for a minute. They won't suspect you."

I needed the money and it sounded real easy. Like he said, they would think Deon's punk ass did it. I couldn't wait to tell Stormy he was out.

"That's that nigga J-White over there. Now, that's who we need to rob. The boy got money. Big bank." Twin said, staring. I could almost see the wheels in his head turning.

I didn't want to turn around too soon to make it obvious.

"Can I look?"

"Yeah, he ain't paying attention. White boy right there." He nodded his head in a certain direction.

"I bet he paid for her ass. Don't no white bitch got ass like that." He frowned.

Scanning the area for a white boy. My heart sunk when my eyes landed on Ju. He was with the bitch who came to his house that night,

Amber. I didn't notice her ass that night. It was big. My breathing sped up. Was my brother talking about Ju?!

"Who?"

"The one with the red hat. Goofy ass nigga don't even look like he got money."

"How you know he got money?" I asked. Still staring not believing what my brother was saying at the same time pissed he was with her.

"Yeah. He owns Dyce. Royal. And Boss. They say him and his brothers are the plug, but I don't know about that. I know he owns the clubs tho. Surprise you don't know him."

"I know him," I mumbled. Dyce was tatted on his stomach. The clubs my brother named were popping, everyone wanted to pop their ass in one of those clubs.

"You do?"

"Yeah. Well not really. He goes to my school."

"J White go to your school?" he hiked a brow.

"Yeah."

"Rich ass don't need school."

My heart broke into a million pieces. I felt so betrayed. He didn't trust me enough to reveal the real him. He lied to my face. That shit hurt thinking about how he must've viewed me as someone beneath him.

"I guess the saying is true, when you rich you play broke and broke play rich. That's why they stay broke." I quoted some shit I read on Facebook. I wanted to cry so bad. I couldn't believe Ju.

"Yup." Twin stood up. "I'm ready to go. This shit nasty and you acting like it's good." He says referring to our food.

I frowned up my face; my stomach was in knots . Nodding my head up and down to agree, I could feel the shit coming up in my throat. I took off toward the restroom. Luckily it was right by where we sat. Pushing a lady out the way and bumping into a baby stroller almost falling over it, I managed to make it to a stall and threw up. My bro was right, I mean the food tasted good going down but was nasty as fuck coming up.

As I rinsed my mouth in the sink, I wondered what Ju thought when he saw past my pretty face and sexy body. I hate to admit it but he hurt my feelings.

I walked over to the pizza place and ordered a Sprite. My brother was sitting at the table across from where I was sitting; it looked like he was having an intense conversation over the phone. I couldn't wait to get back over there and see what that was all about. I didn't play about my brother.

Feeling the vibration coming from my Fanny pack, I pulled the phone out and answered.

"Hey Candy." I haven't talked to her in a week. I smiled glad to hear from her.

"Don't hey me, I know you got my text."

"I did, last night. I forgot." I took the phone off my ear to read her message.

"I was sleep. No, I haven't talked to her since she left for Fiji."

"That ain't like her not to call or text." Candy said.

"Maybe the service is bad out there," I replied not thinking anything of it. Candy and I both knew when Stormy was with Blake, she didn't talk to us as much.

"I don't know, because when I text her, she responds even if it's just to say hey."

I rolled my eyes at Candy's comment. She was forever trying to insinuate that my sister and her relationship was more than what it is. Now, I love Candy, when my sister introduced us as cousin's I accepted her as my cousin . I peep fake shit and feel like she was low key jealous of the bond that my sister and I developed.

While on the phone with Candy I sent a text to my sister asking her to let me know that she was alright.

"I texted her, if she responds I will let you know. I'm about to finish chopping it up with twin."

"Ok. Tell twin I said hey." She smiled. "Let me know if she calls. I know they were to come back today so I may stop by. Knowing Blake, he done pissed her off and she doesn't want to be bothered."

"Right. Talk later. Love you."

"Love you too," she replied, and we ended our call.

After taking a few gulps from my Sprite, I tossed that shit in the nearest trashcan. I didn't even have enough energy to request my $2.25 back. The soda tasted like fucking soda water; dumb mutha fuckas forgot to put the syrup in it.

"You ready twin?" I asked, grabbing my two Macy's bags from the empty chair next to me.

"Yeah, bitch. Who pissed you off?" he slid his phone in his pocket,

"I ain't mad just ready to go, tired." He gave me a knowing look. As my twin, he was always the first to know when something was wrong with me. My mood did change. Aside from vomiting, I was suddenly feeling annoyed.

"Let me find out a nigga got you in your feelings." He raised a brow.

"Please." I turned to walk off, glancing over at the last spot I saw Ju and his chick. "Candy said hi. She called looking for Stormy."

"Oh, your sister?" He tossed.

Twin was another one who felt some kind of way about me and Stormy's relationship. As if she came and stole me from him when the nigga lived in Baltimore. I hardly talked to him.

" She's your sister too. Look at them," I said pointing at the two Tranny's in front of us.

"What about them?" he asked. I detected a little attitude.

"Nothing. If you don't see anything wrong." I shrugged my shoulders. He had taken the fun out of it.

"Our brother is gay. I ain't knocking nothing that makes the next happy."

I didn't even respond. It wasn't that deep for me. It ain't like we didn't clown people on a regular. Now, all of a sudden, he wanted to exclude gays.

Julius

"Get to Cali now. Meeting." Boss demanded.

"What's the problem?" I asked, nudging Amber letting her know that our day at the mall was over.

"The other day some nigga ran up in Big Momma's crib, pistol whipped her. One of the fuck niggas even raped her, bro." I could tell it was hard for my brother to talk about it. Big Momma, was like an aunt to us all. Her and her old man have been supplying the projects ever since I could remember. The couple was initially hired when my big bro Lloyd was in the game. Most of all our old-timers were Lloyd's folks. When Big Momma's husband died a few years ago, I was looking for her to walk away from the hustle; she had enough money to get up out the ghetto, but she refused. She loved what she said was her calling.

"What the fuck happened?" I asked.

"Niggas told her they wanted to know her connect. You already know how she roll. I guess they thought they could beat her into a confession. On momma and daddy, it's on. But that ain't it."

I could feel Amber staring, I didn't want to say too much. My blood boiled over . First the shootout. The rape case I gotta get rid of, and now this shit. Yeah, whoever was coming was loud and fucking with the DYCE brothers. That's the wrong way to be.

"How she doing?"

"Lloyd said they fucked her up. Besides her niece, Lloyd ain't letting nobody in there. Your brother on some other shit too."

"He on one, huh?"

"Yeah. Friday some niggas shot up Bishop's spot again. So, he moved him to the north side. Didn't even tell me."

"Why you ain't call and say nothing?"

"Thought your brother would've called since he wanna act like he the boss."

I glanced across the mall, eyes landing on a familiar chick sitting in the food court with some nigga. Toya's mutha fucking ass.

"Is that," I mumbled.

"Yeah, that's her," I said aloud and then turned and looked at Amber. She frowned as she stared at Toya.

'Fuck her,' I thought. We stepped onto the elevator. Boss was still talking, I tuned back in.

"He what?" I yelled. Boss's revelation had a nigga shocked.

"You heard me. Lloyd said he's stepping back in. I told the nigga we didn't need him. He got the nerve to say, he ain't about to sit back while some niggas play with his family name."

Boss was waiting for me to respond but I didn't have shit to say. I felt him on that. These niggas was trying us and if big bro thought he needed to get his hands dirty then it must've been really bothering him.

"So, you ain't got nothing to say?"

"Not really. I will be out there. I gotta test tomorrow. I will call him and let him know he must postpone the meeting until after tomorrow."

"Bet." Boss retorted. When he hung up without saying bye, I knew he was mad.

I love my brothers. Love them both the same. But Lloyd I respected and plus that nigga was crazy. I wasn't going to test his hand. When I dropped Amber off, I made up my mind that I was going to fall back on her for a minute. She was getting too clingy. She was going off about me dropping her off so I could be with Toya. The shit sounded stupid. Amber knew me well enough to know I don't check for no bitch. Toya wasn't my business.

Toya

Sitting in front of Family Dollar, my heart was pumping at rapid speed. I could almost taste the beating we were about to put on this bitch. I wish Suppa was with her we would've gotten both them hoes. I was going to give it to Diamond so good all them hoes would feel it. Old bitch. She will think twice about hating and stealing again.

After leaving the mall we went back to my twin's hotel. JuJu had me in my feelings. I was snappy and in need of a drink to calm down. Twin's hotel has a bar. After we both showered, we went down for drinks. I just so happened to run into the bitch I was telling y'all about with the dry ass weave. You know, the one who wanted to make friends just to feel like she fitted in.

I walked up to where she was sitting having a drink and wings. Ignoring the fat old man with her I stepped in her face. She was spooked. I wasn't about to fight her just wanted to check her ass.

"If I was a bully, I would beat your ass. Scary hoe. Who the fuck stole my shit?" I grilled.

"Diamond and Suppa." She spilled.

"Why you didn't say shit when I asked about my things?" I know why she didn't I was marking her out on purpose.

"I'm scared of them too." She looked at me like I should know why.

"What you mean too?"

"You scared."

"No, the fuck I'm not. I didn't want to get jumped." I corrected her.

By now my brother walked up and was standing beside me. He had one hand on his hip. I didn't like that.

"What's up. We fucking somebody up?" Twin asked, mad dogging nappy weave.

"I'll tell you later."

"Look," stupid started, " I don't work there anymore. Something bad happened. I know where Diamond works. She works at the Family Dollar until 8pm. I think she's the manager. The one on 30th."

"Who is Diamond?" Twin asked.

"I'll tell you in the car. Come on." I walked off not even thanking the hoe.

On the ride over which wasn't too far from the club, I told twin how them hoes tried to link me, how they hated and stole my shit.

"Why the fuck you just now telling me about them bitches taking your shit twin?" my brother asked animatedly.

I gave him the side eye while thinking he was doing too much with the snake of the neck and shit.

"I wasn't really tripping. I could handle my own but then she stole from me."

"Is that her?" he asked , pointing at this thick chick with a blonde wig.

"No, that's not her. That's her coming out." I grabbed the handle ready to hop out. Twin pulled me back.

"Let me act like I wanna get with her. Walk her to her car and then you get out."

Bet. I watched twin get out of the car. He walked up to ol' girl; whatever he said had her smiling. The girl she was with waived bye and walked off. And like twin said he would, he talked to Diamond while walking her to her car. I hopped out the car, ready to tell that bitch what it was when the next thing you know, I hear screaming coming from across the parking lot. "Bitch, don't you ever motherfucking fuck with my sister!" Twin had slapped Diamond. She stumbled backward and fell to the ground. I took off running across the parking lot; in a flash he was on top of the bitch punching her. "Bitch I will kill you! That's my sister bitch!" I then stepped in, grabbed her by the hair, and slammed her head onto the concrete. We beat the shit out of that hoe.

We laughed all the way back to the hotel. Staring at my brother my heart was suddenly saddened. I'd figure it out. Maybe I always knew. His feminine ways were coming out a little more than usual.

"Bro bro. Are you gay?" I just came out and asked.

He looked at me wiping a fake tear from his eye.

I reached out and hugged him.

"It's nothing to be sad about. I love you."

"Daddy don't." Hearing him say that stung.

"I do. Mom does and so does Von . I'm your twin, don't keep secrets from me. I love you regardless."

"I love you too, hoe."

Candy

Back in Cali

Another day

I know you caught me cheatin and you tired of me lyin,
I'm a be honest witcha baby, I know I crossed the line.
You don't wanna fuck with me no mo then cool, it's fine,
Before you go baby, can we fuck one mo time?

Plies blared from the speakers of my uncle's 64 drop top Chevy. Parked next to him I was posted on the hood of my red Hellcat. Rapping along with one of my favorite rappers. My uncle Moe and his son Itty Bitty was posted next to me rapping along too. Sunday Fun day was a whole vibe. Our car club, along with damn near a hundred others were posted in the shopping center parking lot. The sun was just going down. The police hadn't run us out by now so more than likely this would be our final location for the night.

"Ayee." I smiled, cup in the air feeling good. One more time was my shit. I bumped it so much niggas started calling it my anthem.

I know it's probably best for us to go our separate ways
Cause I know me I'm a fuck up again anyway
But in my muthafuccin heart nigga want you to stay.

I hit myself on the chest singing along.

Itty Bitty was feeling the shit too, " I just had to fuck ya good the other day *And how that pussy was bitin shit ain't wanna escape* *You rode that dick so long until you started to shake."*

We slapped hands. I swear I was the female version of my cousin and uncle. They didn't love these hoes and taught me not to give a fuck about these niggas. I mean I keep it real off back. Most of them understand and those who don't oh fucking well. That nigga Boss tho, the one I've known a few weeks, baby can't seem to understand I'm for the streets!

Let me formally introduce myself. Candy Violet Banks. I'm a twenty-six-year-old high school teacher. I hate my job but at the same time, I love my grown mannish ass students. Aside from teaching, I own a popular low rider parts store. Thanks to my uncle I love low riders. I can't wait until mine is ready. My uncle and my cousin run the shop. They got a whole

191

crew that help with shipping orders. Speaking of them two, besides Grandma they are all the family I have. Uncle Moe is my mother's little brother. They were two years apart. From all the stories that were told they were always close. My mother had me when she was sixteen. My father disappeared right after she told him she was pregnant. My grandmother said momma has always had a selfish spirit and that's why she couldn't believe she wanted to have me, even after her first love left her. I wasn't sure what her reason was either. At eighteen my mom signed over her rights to my grandmother and left to join the army. Almost two years later, she passed away in her sleep. Of course, I don't remember her. My granny, my uncle, and my cousin was all I knew and all I needed. I need my cousin Stormy too. No matter what you learn in this story, just know I love my family.

I continued to vibe to the song. Picking up my cellphone from the side of me, I punched in my password. After checking my text messages and verifying I had no missed calls, I made a mental note to pull-up on Stormy when I left here. I don't know what the fuck is going on with her. Normally when she's in one of her moods she would at least say she was ok and will call me but I heard nothing and it's been three days. Not trying to kill my vibe by thinking the worse, I pumped up Itty Bitty.

"What that nigga Plies say?" We slapped hands again.

"He told the bitch she can go. The pussy good but he ain't going to beg her."

"Right. At least he kept it one hunnid tho." I laughed, taking a gulp from my cup.

"That's why your ass single now. You gonna be forty still trying to play games." The homegirl Dee insinuated.

She pulled up a few minutes ago on her motorcycle. The first thing she did was go over to where her baby daddy was. She was trying to make her presence known cause he was with some chick. That insecure shit is so lame to me.

I responded to her comment, "I don't give a damn if I'm fifty. I will forever be for these streets. Bitch, I ain't you, I don't love these niggas."

Me and Itty-Bitty slapped hands in agreement.

"I can't wait until you eat those words." Dee said, reaching for my cup.

"Make you one." I pointed to the cooler toward the back of the car.

"Aye cuz, who is that?" My uncle inquired.

"No, the fuck it ain't." I mumbled when I laid eyes on the black sports car. The blue flakes were a giveaway.

"That's ol' boy I told you about." I said to Itty Bitty. My phone vibrated in my hand. I already knew it was him,

Boss.

I pressed decline and slid off the car.

"One thing about you, you stay having niggas." Dee called out behind me.

My eyes shot toward Unc who was still glaring at the car.

"You should've made him come to you." He spat.

When I approached the driver's side, the window slowly rolled down.

"What's up?" I smiled, taking in how good he looked and smelled. Those fucking cognac hooded eyes and juicy lips were my weakness. And I'm tipsy too. I really wanted to fuck but a kiss would do. Without even asking I leaned my head into the window like we were a couple. I barely even knew dude but those damn lips.

"Muah." I made a kissing sound.

"Stop playing with me Violet."

"What the fuck dude." I snapped, "Stop calling me that, it ain't cool."

The day we ate at the restaurant I left my purse. I learned he was the owner when he pulled up to my granny's house with my purse. It was a Saturday, the day we chilled at granny's house, and she fried fish. I was so mad when she invited him in.

"You up here in these niggas faces but can't return my call."

"That's my uncle, you remember him. That's my cousin, his son. He had the flu that day you came over."

"The fuck they all staring for, do they know who I am?" He snapped, looking at them then back at me.

I cackled.

"What you mean?"

"I don't know what's funny Violet," he laughed.

I mushed him the head.

"I'm chilling right now with my folks. I'm going to call you." I called myself strutting off. The nigga must've flew up out of his whip. He grabbed me by the arm, turned me around to face him, and pulled me into a hug. His strong hands caressed my back.

"You smell good," I admitted looking up at him.

Boss eased his face closer to mine and just like I did him in the car he stole a kiss. He slid his tongue into my mouth. What the fuck had come over me I don't know. There's no one I would allow this type of affection in public. Fuck it, I didn't have the willpower to stop what was going on between us anyway. I was putty in his hands. Boss was the first to break our kiss. It was quick but he did what he sought out to do. The nigga left me stuck. He had the nerve to flash a smile.

"I be right back." Watching him walk off toward my folks I low key panicked. Boss dapped my uncle up. They exchanged a few words. Unc looked at me as Boss made his way to Dee. He threw his head up to her to say what's up. She smiled and spoke back. The two exchanged a couple of words and he gave her a hug. By the time he made it to Itty Bitty, I had one hand on my hip. The two shook hands. Now, I am standing there waiting for him to bring his ass back over to me.

I could feel all eyes on me. I ain't never been the one out here like Boss had me. I know Dee's ass was about to clown. I will let her have it because I slipped. It will be the last time, I did tho. I rolled my eyes when she came by me.

"Who is that Ms. Playa?" Dee asked.

"You didn't ask him?" I snapped back.

"No, but do he have a brother or an uncle doing it like him?"

I giggled. There was no doubt that his cocky ass was in the big leagues. I've been from the streets all my life. The nigga was doing more than being a restaurant owner. Trust that. I looked at Dee.

"Why you asking? You ain't about to leave that nigga over there." I teased, glancing over at her baby daddy.

A bitch face fell flat when I saw Deon staring at me. His punk ass had the biggest smile on his face like we were cool or some shit.

"Girl, I know Deon ain't out. He looking good too." Dee said.

I rolled my eyes. Seeing his fake ass reminded me I needed to go check on Stormy. As I was about to make my way toward Boss, he was coming my way. He wasn't looking at me though. His hard stare was on whoever was behind me. My gut was telling me who it was because of that death stare. When I looked over my shoulder , he and Deon was mugging each other.

"What's up?" Boss threw his head up, walking right past me.

My heart sank. I stood and watched not sure if I should go have Boss's back or not. Words are being exchanged and with the quickness, I approached the duo.

"Candy, you better tell your boy something." Deon warned.

"Look nigga, don't even say nothing to her. You been watching me like there is a problem since I walked over here. I should've been your first stop if there is an issue. Not right here with these niggas."

"Look, big dog. I don't even know you. I just got out and I ain't trying to go back. You feel me?" Deon looked Boss up and down before turning to talk to Dee's baby daddy.

"Yeah. Alright," Boss responded while nodding his head. His eyes landed on me, "Let's roll."

I gave the nigga a look like, who said I was going anywhere. He shot me one back with raised eyebrows and all. I followed him as he walked off. When we approached his car, I told him.

"I gotta work tomorrow, plus I need to go check on my cousin. I haven't talked to her in a few days."

"I'll take you." He walked up on me pulling me into his arms.

"You gotta stop doing that."

"What, letting niggas know when I'm out here you belong to me?"

"You wild my nigga."

Licking his full lips his eyes peered into mine.

"I wanna hit that pussy again. One time wasn't enough. And after that, it still won't be enough."

He didn't even know how wet he had me. I wanted to fuck his good dick having ass too. I been craving his sex since that night. A bitch strong tho, I held out from calling him.

"After I check on my cousin, I can meet you somewhere."

"Nah, I am going to take you to check on your peoples, then we can go back to your place."

"We ain't going over my house. Nigga I don't know you." I laughed, "and I wanna check on my girl by myself."

He broke our embrace. The annoyed look on his face had me feeling some kind of way.

"Bye." I tossed.

"Bet." He hit me with a reverse nod and opened his car door.

"Bossss! Bossss!" A group of females sang. Looking in the direction of the thirsty ass voices I saw that it was the Range Rover crew. Their car club consisted of wanna be bougie bitches. Leaving his door open he met the hoes halfway. He embraced the first two with a friendly hug. The other hoe he pulled into his arms almost holding her like he held me and then whispered in her ear. When she pulled away, she was smiling big. This nigga walked back over to his car not even looking my way but had the nerve to say bye to Dee. He jumped in the car and pulled up on the bitches. I walked over to my own car and hopped in. I was going to check on Stormy. As I was pulling off Dee ran up to my car and told me one of the hoes got in the car with him. I gave her a reverse nod and pulled off. I know my uncle and Itty Bitty was going to clown my ass. I didn't even say bye.

I swerved in and out of traffic in silence thinking about how Boss played me. I couldn't wait to see that nigga again so I could stunt on his black ass. He did that though. He got the wrong one because I can play the game just as good if not better than the next nigga. Enough of him being on my mind. I turned on my radio and let the music play.

I hated her ass lived so far but whatever, I had to go make sure my girl was cool. The sun dipped off and now I had to go up this dark ass hill. It was only a two-way road. So, if your shit broke down while driving you were fucked.

Deon's lame ass crossed my mind. I thought about whether or not I should tell Stormy that he was out. She hated his guts. I couldn't stand him either. He was a sneaky, grimy ass nigga. My uncle told me that word on the streets was he is the snake that stole her father's drugs that resulted in her mother getting killed. I don't know if Stormy knows or if it even matters why but I know she hated her father and considered him the one that pulled the trigger on her mother.

My cellphone rang through my Bluetooth. The caller ID displayed Beverly Hills PD. My first thought was to let the shit go to voicemail.

"Yeah." I answered, turning the music down.

"It's me, Stormy." She cried.

My fucking heart dropped. A bad feeling washed over me.

"Stormy where are you? I'm going up the hill to your house now."

"In jail. I need you to bail me out. I have the money."

"In jail?" I yelled.

I don't know if I was more pissed off that I had to go up this got damn hill before I could turn around and go get her . Or the fact that she just told me she was in jail.

"What in the hell happened?" I asked, pressing on the gas trying to hurry up. "Hello. Hello." I looked at the screen on my dash and realized the call dropped. Fuck. I gotta get to Stormy.

Lloyd

I was chilling in my backyard puffing a cigar and having a glass of cognac. Jamie was taking her nightly swim. She was naked and wanted me to join her. I asked her to give me a minute. I was going to join her and fuck the shit out of her. I had a lot of tension to release.

The last few weeks, I 've been dealing with a lot of unnecessary stress. I hated stress. I am a believer that you are in control of what you allow to affect you. My pops would always say, if you allow unwanted feelings to control your life then you are a coward. A man not only fights for his possessions, his life, and the people he loves, he fights for peace of mind. No situation or person should have so much control over your life.

And that's why I am getting back into the game. Whoever these punks are coming for DYCE must be eliminated. There was no way I could sit back and allow these niggas to get clout off my family's blood, sweat, and tears.

I tossed back my glass finishing the last of my Remy. Then I placed my cigar into the ashtray on the patio table. After stripping out of my clothes I made my way to the pool and dove in. The water was warm just how I liked it at night. Off back, I did a lap around the pool. Images of Fiji and the woman I spent time with invaded my thoughts. No matter how much I tried to forget about the beautiful Stormy I couldn't. But. It was a must. With me stepping back into the game any chances of us messing around were over. I know before I said I just wanted to fuck and move on but the moment I saw her a second time I knew just a fuck wouldn't be enough. Stormy didn't have to tell me she wasn't a fan of hustlers. The comment that punk ass Blake made told me what I needed to know. She was already fucking with a fuck nigga. Everyone but her knew that Blake had a woman and a child. Whenever she found out I knew she would be heartbroken. The way she spoke on him I knew she believed she had someone special. Knowing that I couldn't give her what she deserved I stepped off.

Coming from under the water my eyes landed on Jamie. With a smile on her face, she summoned me with her finger to come to her. The woman was beautiful. Sexy. And loved me deeply. I dove back under the warm water swimming to her. I rose from the water lifting her up by her waist. Jamie wrapped her legs around me. Hungrily she attacked my mouth. With every step I took to get her near the wall my dick stiffened.

"Ahh." She gasped when I rammed my pole into her. "Can you make love to me?" She pleaded, causing me to look into her hopeful eyes. Covering her mouth back with mine I stroked her a little slower than normal until I busted.

The two of us showered together and she topped me off. I enjoyed sex with my fiancé always have but it was Stormy who I couldn't stop thinking about. After the shower, Jamie served me steak and a baked potato in bed. I didn't even know I had fallen asleep until I was awakened by the same nightmare I've been having for years. Getting up from the bed, I decided to go workout in my home gym.

Michelle is calling. Alexa announced. Besides being Jamie's aunt, she is my accountant. When she wasn't getting on my nerves she was working.

"That mutha fucka. I swear I'm going to kill him." Her voice slurred.

"Kill who? And why are you telling me?"

"Blake. I am going to kill him. I'm telling you because I have no one else who will bail me out."

I chuckled.

"What are you talking about? Why would you wanna kill your best friend's son."

It didn't matter to me if he lived or died. But why did Michelle want him dead?

"That cheating son of a bitch. He had the nerve. And his punk ass father. He's so busy being in his son's business when he needs to be worried about how his wife is fucking every black dick from here to the Netherlands."

"Michelle." I couldn't stop laughing. "What did them people do to you?"

"He fucked with my family. My got damn family. I didn't do right by her mother. My baby was killed without knowing I loved her." She began to cry.

I was confused but I listened.

"Blake hit Stormy over the head. She's in the hospital but in custody. He hit my granddaughter in the head. He's dead. I swear he will pay." She sobbed.

"WHAT?" Jamie and I say in unison. I didn't even know she was behind me.

The phone hung up.

.

Julius

Ding:

My phone went off letting me know I had a text.

My bad, I apologized to my brother. We were sitting at the round table in his office about to have a meeting. Putting my phone on silent I pulled up the text icon and saw the message was from Toya. Wasn't even fucking with her no more not even sure why she even reached out. I wished she wouldn't. After seeing her with that nigga, I was cool. Every time you turn around, she is with a different one.

"I am going back to my old connect. I heard a few of the members complain about how our product wasn't as potent as it was when we were dealing with the Asians. Until we find out who is trying to come for us there, we are not allowing any new clients. Our old clients must pay in full, or we will send someone who can take over their territory. And most importantly, we will lay low. And wait. Dumb niggas will think they stopped us and come out from hiding and that's when we strike."

The two of us listened as Lloyd Dyce told us what was what. Nothing he presented seemed like a bad idea. However, I know Boss didn't think the same.

"You saying all this but still ain't explained how you can come back in and take over something you left. When I took the position, I wasn't temporarily holding it down until you felt like you wanted to be a drug dealer again." Boss barked; his face was frowned up. He had a point.

"You think I want back in? I don't want nothing to do with this shit, but since you two niggas just gotta continue the legacy I ain't about to let you fuck up what mom and dad built. No, what I built." He slammed his fist down on the table. "Nobody even knew who we were until your loudmouth ass wanted to make it known."

"What the fuck you mean? Nobody knows I'm in the game. I don't go around broadcasting shit." Boss yelled.

"Mutha fucka you socialize with the block boys. You invited them to the annual Dyce party. That shit was stupid. Everyone ain't dumb like you think. It ain't shit to put two and two together."

"Man, whatever." He fanned his hand, standing up. "Is that it, boss?" he said sarcastically.

Lloyd looked at me.

"You ain't said nothing. Tell me why you think it's ok to supply a nigga whose wife our family killed." He shook his head. "It's stupid shit like that. I don't give a fuck what y'all told him the deal is off the table. I don't trust him."

"Nigga and I don't trust Jamie. Bitch disappeared for two years. Then came back with some lame ass story. How in the fuck are you honoring a promise you made to our father when her own father don't fuck with her? Something ain't right with that bitch but you know everything." Boss said.

Lloyd sat back in his seat and chuckled.

"You should've been said something if you felt like that."

"Wait. What you mean we supplying someone who snaked us before? What you talking about?" I asked.

"So, you didn't tell him, Boss?"

" I ain't had a chance."

"What?" I yelled.
"Nothing because the deal is off, and after we silence these niggas, I am ordering you niggas to walk away from the shit. We are rich, we don't need it."

"I will when I'm ready. I ain't ready, it's the thrill." I replied and shrugged. "Are we done?" They thought what they said was final. I planned on walking away after I finished school, but I will announce it when I'm ready.

"I see y'all tomorrow. It's my birthday remember." Lloyd reminds us.

"We know." Boss and I said in unison.

Every year he wanted to throw a BBQ golf and talk about old times. This year me and Boss were throwing him a party at our club. We were going to have the grand opening the same day.

I'm the nerdy ass white boy as Toya says but I swear my brother was boring. Big Momma said when he finds that right woman, he will be a different person. Jamie wasn't it tho.

We chopped it up a little while longer and bounced. I started to hit up Bishop to let him know I was on my way. However, I changed my mind. My brother told me how he had a lot of niggas loitering where we do business. Now that he was relocated, I wanted to see how he was moving.

I pulled up a few houses down from the spot. I decided I wanted to sit and watch. As I waited, I remembered I had yet to read Toya's message.

Toya: I guess the joke is on me. When I got over the shock I laughed. I'm sure you have your reasons for lying. I mean, who would want a stripper bitch to know anything about them. You probably thought I would set you up. Most people don't trust us black girls no matter how much they claim they fuck with us.

I was with my twin at the mall the other day. He saw you and BECKY!! He told me you own a few of the hottest strips clubs in Cali. He said Baller Alert did an interview on you. That house you lied about is yours huh? The cars too? I know. I'm good enough to fuck without protection tho. I hate you, Bishop!! Bye, stupid lying ugly ass white boy. Fuck you.

Toya

"Why you acting so uneasy baby?" Bishop asked, handing me a drink.

Many reasons, was what I wanted to say but of course, I couldn't. I can tell y'all though. I sent Ju a text, I called myself telling him off about being a got damn liar and done called him another man's name. I waited to see if he would respond but I got nothing. So, now I'm mad at him but at the same time wondering if he's tripping about me calling him Bishop. By the time I leave here I hope I get a text from him. My brother and his boy are coming to run up in here. I ain't new to this. The handful of times I did a job everything went as planned. No one was ever hurt nor suspected I set them up.

Bishop took a seat next to me pulling my leg onto his lap and massaging it.

"I want you to dance for me." He said before planting light kisses on my neck.

"As long as you paying," I replied.

"You already know."

I took my drink to the head, stood up, and excused myself to the restroom. I texted my brother letting him know the door was unlocked. I told him to wait thirteen minutes before coming in. I felt by the time we were into the second song I would have his dick in my mouth. Bishop would be in another world and when they run in on him, being in such a vulnerable state will make things easier.

I turned on Shake That Monkey as I stripped out of my clothes keeping on my lace G string. I stay smelling good, but I still sprayed a little body spray on. I left my bag in the restroom and came out holding my phone in the air moving to the song.

The fool had turned all the lights on but whatever. Niggas loved looking at my sexy body.

Singing along with the song I turned into the living room... Ready to put on a show.

"BITCH WHO SENT YOU?" The familiar voice roared.

My eyes widened panic took over. Julius was in the living room with a gun pointed at me.

"Oh my god. Oh my god." I didn't know whether to cover my breasts or my mouth.

"Who sent you?" He growled.

He acted like he didn't even know me.

"I'm going to ask you one more time."

"J white she ain't on that." Bishop jumped in. "This my bitch. Take the gun off her."

Ju gave me a death stare as he chuckled. I stood there not knowing what to do or say. The tears just wouldn't stop coming. My heart felt like it was going to jump out my chest. I started to feel sick. I fucked up.

I began to step back as Ju walked toward me. His gun was still aimed at my head.

"You think I won't kill you, Toya? You trying to rob me bitch?"

To be continued...

Please post a review. Your feedback, thoughts, and support are needed. Part two the Finale will drop no later than 5/1.

Have you read Saved by His Hood Love 1-3?

Made in United States
North Haven, CT
23 March 2022

17454639R00117